A NobleJay Short Story Collection

Volume Two

Edited by Ellie Jay and Neil Noble

Featuring Stories by Mason Bushell, Ellie Jay, Fleur Lind, Neil Noble, Robert Mackey, Betty Mermelstein, Alec Sillifant and Pamela Smith

ISBN (e-book): 978-1-0683321-6-6

ISBN (paperback): 978-1-0683321-7-3

Table of Contents

Introductory Content

Stories

Meet The Authors

Here, you can find the biographies of all the writers who contributed to this anthology, along with links to their prior works and social sites where you can find them. If you particularly enjoy a writer's content, we highly recommend browsing their other works.

Mason Bushell

Mason Bushell is a classically trained chef and bartender who's worked in a top hotel chain. His most rewarding venture in the hospitality industry was serving the veterans of the Royal British Legion.

In between times, he learned to decorate cakes and supported many people with their birthday and wedding plans. He is an amateur wildlife photographer and is never out without his camera around his neck. He loves spending time exploring the woods and countryside with his dog in tow. Mason has always been into books. His parents ensured he read every day from a very young age. His family and teachers always remember him as the boy with the big book under his arm. His first memory of enjoying writing came from English class. He would be given the title of a story he had to write as an assignment. His classmates would hand in a half page at best. Meanwhile, captivated by his characters, Mason would pen an entire adventure many pages long.

As he moved through school and entered college to become a chef, Mason strayed from writing for a while. It wasn't until his grandmothers both became ill with cancer that he found solace in the fantasy world he created. Then whilst working at the hotel, his head chef inadvertently showed him a short story competition advert in the newspaper. The thrill of a mystery story grabbed his imagination and set about some magical events. Even though she wasn't in the story, he would meet a special sleuth called Holly.

The meeting was so profound it forced him to take time off work to write what became the start of a seven-year journey into the mystery world. Even though he failed Holly, and her series will not be available to the public, Mason still writes short stories when the desire takes him. He hopes you will find a smile in those stories and join him in his Menagerie for a read when you can.

masonsmenagerie.wordpress.com

Works by Mason can be found on pages 33-51, 149-157 and 207-218.

Ellie Jay

Ellie Jay is an independent author with a love of fiction and a nasty habit of sarcasm. She writes books of all different genres and ties them all together with sarcastic third-person narration.

At the moment, her published works include The Secrets Series, a trilogy of Russian Mafia action thrillers with dashes of sci-fi and overarching sarcasm and Planet of Lies, a sci-fi story that is packed full of witty dialogue and narration. She has also produced a three-in-one special edition of The Secrets Series, and had work published in the anthologies Quick Stories and Poems Volumes 1 and 2.

She also dabbles in book reviews, author advice, social media marketing and more. She is focusing on polishing her brand and growing all the avenues she works within, including the editing, compiling and publication of anthologies and collections such as this one.

Ellie Jay also comprises one half of Noble Jay, a fledgling alliance of indie authors Ellie Jay and Neil Noble, who intend to continue creating collections that showcase many more great short stories.

You can find Ellie's prior works here:
https://www.amazon.com/stores/author/B08XC1CVMG or connect directly at @EllieJayWrites on Twitter/X to learn more.

Works by Ellie can be found on pages 105-125.

Neil Noble

Author Neil Noble was born in Washington DC. Throughout his teenage years he developed an interest in politics which led him to participate in demonstrations "against" the Vietnam war and "for" integration, equal rights and equal pay movements. At the age of 15, he was part of the crowd at the Lincoln Memorial where he heard Dr. King's "Dream" speech.

He and his wife Betty will celebrate their 45th wedding anniversary in October. Neil has many interests outside of writing. Some of these interests include art, antiques, biblical history, music composition, and travel. He is interested in everything and fascinated by whatever is left over. All his pursuits contribute to his work in some way.

His back list includes a book of illustrated poetry that was released in March 2019. He has been published in two different anthologies; one for his poetry and one for his short stories (both in 2021). He was interviewed on two different live podcasts; one in Baltimore, Maryland and one in London, England.

He is currently finishing a fictional novella related to Buddhism, a second book of illustrated poetry, more short stories, a lecture series on the Dead Sea Scrolls, and an animated movie script based on the Christmas story but from a dog's point of view. When time permits, he still writes and composes songs, most of which can be found on social media sites such as Youtubemusic.com and Spotify.com.

You can find Neil's books by typing the ISBNs into Google.

9798458788052 for his poetry anthology

9781666272451 for his short story anthology

9798603555850 for Moods of a Lake and Selected Poems

Works by Neil can be found on pages 17-32, 140-149, 199-206 and 266-272.

Betty Mermelstein

Betty Mermelstein has had a variety of articles, poems, short stories, and humorous essays published, as well as having self-published books for children and adults, along with a published children's book. Much of her work is based on her own life experiences, whether they are childhood memories, traveling experiences, or love of her natural surroundings. She lives in the Phoenix area of Arizona where she and her husband enjoy spending time with their sons' families, traveling, biking, and kayaking. Betty is a retired teacher and avid ballroom dancer.

Works by Betty can be found on pages 52-56, 158-166 and 219-224.

Robert Mackey

Robert Mackey resides in, near really, the pathetic excuse for a hamlet, Addy Washington. Robert has done everything in his power not to contribute to excellence in writing or even advance shoddiness in writing. He did, however, manage to fail at this endeavor by creating a trilogy of outlandish, ludicrous, adventure tales for the young and young at heart.

These works are free of killing, sex and profanity. This was no accident. Robert thought this a good idea after reading The Hunger Games series, something of which his nine-year-old son and his friends could not get enough. Robert felt kids killing kids for food and the amusement of adults to be something less than appropriate for, well, anyone really.

Having changed the world for the better with said works, Robert had apparently decided it was time to toss out a few profane, insane, inane and any other words rhyming with train, works, for the kids he saved from the horrors and irresponsible messages delivered by the mainstream entertainment industry. These kids have grown into intelligent, although a bit too sensitive, adults by now and must be toughened up a bit.

So, we now have his works for adults who might get offended by things not politically correct, profane, or just completely absurd. Robert feels these novels should help these happy-go-lucky, loving souls, assimilate into the rough-and-tumble world in which we all must live. So, to use a lead in which seems popular to chronic, lying politicians, make no mistake, Robert has written something for everyone, except Ghandi, 'cause he read most everything during his life and doesn't need saving from, or help assimilating into society, because, well, he's dead. Namaste, happy birthday, and *GO ZAGS!*

You can find Robert's books here:

Something the Matter in Hell: Mybook.to/hell

Hard Way Out: Mybook.to/hardwayout

Trouble With Howlers: Mybook.to/howlers

Trouble on the High Seas: Mybook.to/highseas

Trouble Down Under: Mybook.to/downunder

The Other Side of the Wall: Mybook.to/othersidewall

Works by Robert can be found on pages 87-93, 167-179 and 225-251.

Pamela Smith

Pamela Smith is an Army veteran, summa cum laude graduate with a Bachelor's in English with Honors from Florida Atlantic University, and lover of all things English and literature.

She has written multiple short stories, specializing in Young Adult and New Adult fiction, various poems, and is currently working on her first book. For her short story, 'Golden Girl', she enjoyed taking a well-known concept and adding a twist to make it her own.

She now writes for Winter is Coming, which is all about fantasy, and will be mainly specializing in Harry Potter.

A Christian, she thanks God for an opportunity to share her work, as well as her family, including her four dogs, for their encouragement and support.

You can find Pamela's works here:

https://www.fau.edu/artsandletters/english/honors-programs/english-honors/honors-spotlight-2024-pamela-smith/

https://coastlinesfau.wordpress.com/wp-content/uploads/2024/12/coastlines-2024.pdf

Or follow her at all.things.pamela on Instagram

Works by Pamela can be found on pages 57-86.

Alec Sillifant

Alec Sillifant likes to think of himself as a writer…he also likes to think of himself as 22 years old, but life doesn't work that way.

In the past he has had some success with several picture books, a couple of young reader chapter books and a YA novel being published. These are no longer in print, and each was woefully, and unjustifiably, lacking in awards and worldwide acclaim. He thinks there may still be time for all that to change…there isn't.

Alec has also busted his chops for many a decade as a copywriter for the greetings card industry. Some of his work may well have graced a table/mantelpiece/windowsill you own. Just think, you may have been called an 'old git' via proxy by a seriously underrated literary genius.

He also writes under the pen name 'Sif' and has self-published three books. The first being a collection of short stories that featured in custom motorcycle magazines back in the 1990s and are loosely based on his teenage years…very, very loosely. The other two volumes are collections of short, humorous essays that deal with all the small annoyances in the modern world that get his (Sif's) goat. Imaginatively titled, 'Sif Rants' and 'Sif Rants Again', these books have already upset at least one marathon runner to his knowledge. He hopes to upset many more people in the days to come.

Lately he has been going back to his roots and writing fiction for the custom motorcycle magazine, *Back Street Heroes'* whilst also working on the epitaph for his gravestone which will, like all his scribbling, be in dire need of grammar and punctuation corrections. So, if you know anyone willing…

Works by Alec can be found on pages 126-139, 180-198 and 259-265.

Fleur Lind

Fleur Lind is from New Zealand. She and her husband moved to rural SE Queensland 10 years ago. Fleur works in Community Aged Care and enjoys writing short stories with a quirky twist.

Fleur is the author of a story/memoir, Blarney to Bastille - A Kiwi on Cobblestones. It tells of her first trip to the UK and Europe in 2019. Filled with first-time experiences, it embraces everything about living a 40-year-old dream, without Googling it first.

You can find Fleur at all the links below:

Fleursfabulousfables.wordpress.com

Facebook.com/Addicted2Writing

Twitter.com/AutorFleurL

Works by Fleur can be found on pages 94-104, 252-258 and 273-284.

THE VIGILANTES

By Neil Noble

I was born and raised in Washington, D.C., and its surrounding Maryland suburbs.

What I remember of the 1960's began with peace and love for all.

I grew up in this decade. Dr. King gave his "I Have a Dream" speech in 1963. He was standing directly in front of the Lincoln Memorial because of the significance of Lincoln's efforts on behalf of people of color. I happened to be standing about 150 feet from him.

The Capitol Building is the hub in the center of Washington. In front of it, and about two miles long, is the National Mall Park. This runs from East to West all the way to the Potomac River. The Washington Monument and the White House are at about the halfway mark of the mall, at the western end is the Lincoln Memorial. Constitution Avenue is on the north side; Independence Avenue is on the south.

Both Lincoln and King spoke about all people being equal. I was 16 in 1963, and I heard King's speech. I believed the words he spoke. I was already thinking that way because I grew up in integrated schools and neighborhoods. Someone's color never even entered my mind. They were just another kid to me.

It was incredibly quiet for a crowd that large. Two hundred and fifty thousand people were present, according to the newspapers. After the speech, I started to walk away, lost in my thoughts, and trying to process and remember what Dr. King said. Someone tapped me on the shoulder. I turned to see two men of color. One looked to be twenty-something, the other had salt and pepper hair. They were surprised that a young, white boy was there and interested in what Dr. King had to say. There were many white people present that day, but I was probably the youngest. The day was sunny, hot, and muggy, normal for summer in Washington.

The three of us walked and talked for a while. Actually, they mostly talked, and I mostly listened. I began to grow up that day. I did not understand some of the things

Dr. King said and I asked about them. The men explained some things and helped me to see a little more clearly. The whole concept of segregation was foreign to me. I knew the history of it. I just didn't understand how and why slavery developed into segregation and was allowed to continue one hundred years after the Civil War. Why was segregation so necessary to the survival of society? Who was afraid of what? The two men patiently explained it all to me. At some point, my age came up. I told them I was 16. I had hitchhiked to D.C. and then walked to the mall.

They patiently answered all the questions I could think of. During our conversation, I mentioned I was Jewish. I knew what they were going through. But I never knew the "why" of it. My ancestors had suffered since the days of Abraham, nearly six thousand years. The older man, Moses, smiled. He was the thoughtful type. I watched him think before he spoke. Maybe he was choosing his words or maybe he was just thinking about his audience of one. When we parted, Moses handed me a piece of paper with a phone number on it. He told me to call the number and tell whoever answered that Moses said to call. I stuck it in my pocket and forgot it.

The Los Angeles race riots, in the summer of 1965 was an unfortunate situation because the powder was already loaded, and the primer set. The spark was when a white cop tried to arrest a black man for a minor driving infraction. That set off the powder keg of pent-up emotions and hatred. The temperature was not the only heat rising that day.

Over the next few years, 159 different cities experienced some degree of race riots. Baltimore and Washington were no exception. They exploded in the summer of 1967, when I was 20. To the best of my knowledge, there was just one difference between this Baltimore-Washington area and the rest of the country. We had a vigilante group, and this was the mission and focus of Moses.

I called the phone number Moses had given me a week or so after our first meeting at the Lincoln Memorial. I was about to throw my jeans into the clothes hamper when I remembered to go through the pockets. The younger black man and I never revealed our names, but Moses gave his people a good description of me. That proved to be necessary and useful later.

When I called, my instructions were to wait at a certain location at a certain time near the Washington Monument. When I got there, I saw a phone booth. Because I watched too much television, I expected the phone to ring to give me another address. I was still by myself at the appointed time. The phone never rang. A half hour passed when a young, white girl walked past and asked me the time. Since I was a healthy teenager, I suddenly had a head full of mush. Here was a cute chick who struck up a conversation with *me*. Being shy and somewhat introverted, my mouth was full of cotton, my eyes were starting to drift down below her face and certain mechanical actions became enhanced, which she obviously noticed. She giggled a bit then took pity on me and told me she was the contact I was to meet. My mouth was still full of cotton, but I was now awake and alert.

We walked for a few minutes and sat down on a park bench to talk. Our entire conversation was about equal rights, the state of current politics and society, in general. My folks encouraged me to read the newspaper and not just the comics and sports. I was too naïve to think to ask questions like why all this cloak and dagger stuff? Who are you? To what group do you belong? Is this a job interview?

After about 45 minutes, she finally said, "You'll do." As she got up to walk away, she said over her shoulder, "Call the same number in a week and tell them Moses said to call again."

That was that. I still had no answers, nor would I, until I called a second time. When I did, someone gave the phone to Moses. He invited me to come over to meet the rest of the team.

This time, I was more functional, and I said "No, not until I know more about you and your 'team.' What do you want with me? Why are you interested in me? Who are you?"

Moses was patient with me.

"It's okay if you don't trust me; we can meet in some public place. How about the same place where you met with Martha?"

At that moment, I realized she and I never exchanged names. I was too busy trying to see through the fog in my head.

"I'll arrange for some of my people to join at half-hour intervals to avoid suspicion."

"To avoid suspicion", I replied, "does not help me trust you more."

"Relax," Moses said, "all that's going to happen is just a conversation so the others can get to know a little about you. I am trying to recruit you to join my mission, and I'll explain it to you when we sit and talk."

And that's what happened. We met at the Washington Monument about mid-morning, a couple of days later. It was more pleasant than the first time we met. There was a light breeze, and it was partly cloudy.

Moses arrived and sat to my left while an older white man sat to my right. As the three of us sat and talked about King, his work and society in general, three or four other people came and went. They all participated in some part of our conversation. The conversation had to do with the violence simmering in each city where there were demonstrations. I asked about the violence.

Moses explained he was the recruiter, and the other man was the coordinator. The white man seldom spoke but did listen intently. Their combined jobs were to do something about the violence when it came to the Baltimore-Washington area. Not 'if' but 'when'.

When I mentioned the violence again, the two men looked at each other and smiled.

The older white man then asked, "Would you join in and help us?"

His voice was deep and strong and no-nonsense.

Although not introduced, I did soon learn his name; 'Captain.'

Over the next few weeks, I met with Moses and the Captain several times. They had been intentionally vague with me in the beginning, as a test. They were trying to determine the level of my commitment to their cause. I passed and joined the 'team.' As a group, we intended to disrupt the bad element mixed in with the demonstration for the greater good of its intent.

In any given civil demonstration, there are always opportunists trying to take advantage of the general confusion to loot and steal. We were Vigilantes trying to limit the damage done for a good cause. Civil Disobedience was the propaganda name given to rioting, which has a negative connotation. Because of my age, I stayed with Moses doing whatever he asked, as we prepared for the inevitable clash.

There were 52 active participants in total. There were also two or three much older men on the phone or doing other clerical work in our 'office,' which was the living room of someone's apartment. There were three brigades, each consisting of sixteen men and women.

They varied in age from late teens to early twenties and were of mixed races. Each brigade had a leader, a Lieutenant. Four sergeants further divided each brigade into four squads of four. I have no idea if anyone used his or her real name. Nobody seemed to care and that was probably for the best. A Captain led this whole group. That was his only name. Yes, it was the same Captain I had met.

One brigade always stayed in Baltimore. Their leader was Lieutenant Mason. Another group always stayed in Washington. Lieutenant Dixon was in charge there. Lieutenant Rover led the last group, held in reserve. The Captain did use them frequently. He made 52; three brigades of sixteen people plus three lieutenants and our Captain.

I don't know for sure, but I think Moses and the Captain saw the humor in our location and the names of our leaders, Mason and Dixon. Nobody cared about names; it made things safer and simpler for everyone. Each Lieutenant carried a roll of dimes and called a phone number several times a day to communicate with the Captain. They would give him their current location, and he would tell them where the police and National Guard were. The demonstration began at the Lincoln Memorial and moved East toward the Capitol building. Rioting followed behind.

The newspapers only referred to it as Civil Disobedience; to use the word 'riot' might imply that authority figures were not in control of the situation. They did what they needed to do when called to a specific location, but most of the time, they were part of the perimeter or patrolling a beat outside of the perimeter.

In 1967, I was in college in Baltimore. I was very much involved in planning and moving people around. None of us were caught. I can't say the same for the bad people.

We mixed and blended in with demonstrators in both cities. Whenever we saw a small group break off, a few of us would offer to go along. We knew they planned to loot one or more stores because they were a small group, and they headed in a different direction than the protesters. Most of the time we let them break the windows to gain entrance to a store. Occasionally, we helped. It did feel good to break a big plate glass window. In any case, two of our squad members would enter the store with the looters and the other two would stay outside offering to be lookouts.

When they came out, we would jump one or two stragglers and tie them to a telephone pole, lamppost or whatever was nearby. One of us would pin a note to each person caught and then leave the stolen goods beside him or her. The notes simply said, "I stole this stuff."

Then we would call the cops to pick them up. Eventually, word got around, and we ended up being hunted by both the cops, for doing their job, and by the rioters for calling the cops, 'dropping a dime' on them.

By the time our company disbanded, I was Lieutenant Mason. In 1972, I moved to San Francisco, mostly for my own safety. I never told my folks what I was doing although they said they watched it all on T.V.

The irony of this chapter of my life was the very act of moving to San Francisco. On the same block of California Street, I lived in a humble apartment, down the hill, while at the other end, atop Nob Hill, in their spacious condo, was the Hearst family. The Symbionese Liberation Army kidnapped the daughter, Patty, in 1974.

There were reporters parked everywhere. The police had blocked that section of the street to limit access. I had to show identification every time I returned home after work. I was trying to keep a low profile and couldn't. But nothing ever happened. I never told my wife about my history either.

I tried to call Moses to see if he could put me in touch with people out west. I found out he had moved on to the next probable hotspot and I never saw or heard from him again. I moved back East in 1978 after my divorce. I still haven't run into any familiar faces. Isn't it a curious thing about hiding in plain sight?

Since that first day, I have tried, to actively practice what Dr. King preached. Equal rights, for everyone, are a difficult concept to understand and even more difficult to put into practice. It is getting better now, but racism still manages to rear its ugly head, even today.

One cannot judge history by present-day morality. That is comparing apples to oranges. The right or wrong of history depends on the customs and morals of society, at the time. Every demonstration for civil rights, throughout the history of our Republic, has been about hatred, ignorance, and violence. Even the police actively participate. We are *all* immigrants. Ignorance and hatred are the parents of bigotry.

HIS WORDS

I heard a man speak in D.C. today; I heard him say "you cannot delay"

His words seemed meant just for me; so far ahead of his time was he.

His words came from his prophet's soul; we are almost to our Promised Land goal

Simple, straightforward, and very clear; they clung so fiercely to my ear.

Behind him sat the one who set the path; his words created so much wrath

I know his words and am compelled; and yet that division must be quelled.

Half a million lives were lost; for four long years were state lines crossed

Until, at last, the General's words agreed; "all our nation needs to be freed."

Their words were indeed very fine, but actual change must still be defined

We need to figure out what needs doing now; there's still more work to do somehow

Any solution will be far too rare; making it work would be a nightmare

Plus another generation to have any effect; someone's words will argue a hurtful defect.

A FLOATING SIGNAL FOR HELP

By Mason Bushell

"Rescue Base to Rescue One. Lynn or Denzel, do you copy?"

"This is Lynn. Go ahead, Erica, over."

She glanced through her steaming breath at a golden eagle soaring over the snowy mountains above her and smiled. Mountain Rescue was the best job.

"We found the boys exploring the Ministry of Defense Airfield. They're safe but in a mountain of trouble."

"Ouch! Roger that, we'll head for home." Lynn hopped upon the trunk of a fallen beech tree and looked at her partner. "You hear that, Denz? We can head back."

A rugged man with salt and pepper hair and chiseled features, Denzel looked like he belonged in the forest aside from his orange rescue coat. Frozen to the spot, he said nothing.

"Hey, Denz!" Lynn called louder, frosty snow crunched beneath her boots as she approached him.

"Sorry. What do you make of that?" He pointed between spruce trees to the mountain lake.

Its mirror surface reflected the trees and white mountain. Beauty marred by five orange row boats drifting, forlorn and empty.

"Hmm, that's odd. They're tied together and adrift. They'll be Spruce Bruce's hire boats, right?"

Denzel nodded. "I believe so. He shut for winter on the 31st of October to beat the treacherous weather."

"He wouldn't leave his boats on the water then, would he?" Lynn followed him toward the lakeside.

"No, something's wrong. He has a shed for winter storage which means either someone sabotaged his boats or …"

"He's sending an S.O.S." Lynn felt her rescue pack grow heavier as the situation's gravity pressed against her. "Whose swimming after the boats?"

"Sod that! It's -4 Centigrade out here. Those boats are empty and floating fine for now." Denzel pointed a glove to the south. "We need to get to Bruce's place."

"Agreed, Come on."

The two rescuers jogged along the shore with the mountain to their backs.

"Rescue base, this is Lynn."

"Go ahead for base, over." Erica's voice sounded distant on the radio.

"We've found five of Spruce Bruce's boats adrift. Going to check his place now."

'Roger that, I'll try to call him."

"Thanks, we'll keep you updated."

Lynn exchanged a glance with Denzel. They were both apprehensive.

Soon the white-painted jetty of Spruce Bruce's day hire came into view, jutting from the rocky shore into the lake. Two small shacks on shore were the kiosk and shop.

"Those boats should be in there."

Denzel pointed beyond the shacks and car park to the cedar-boarded storage shed. He was leant against and peering around a pine tree with his binoculars.

"So, why were they adrift in the lake?" Lynn said, hiding behind a beech tree. Even watching a pair of majestic moose graze on the high meadow did little to calm her nerves now.

"I don't know. There are no cars and it's quiet."

"Too quiet if those boats have anything to say." Lynn focused on her partner. "What's our move?"

"Base to Rescue One, over."

"Go ahead, Erica," Denzel said exhaling a cloud of steam into the frigid air.

"Bruce's phone is going unanswered. I can't reach him at home or on his mobile."

"That means his family isn't answering either," Lynn noted.

"Thanks, Erica. Call the police, please. We're at his jetty now. We'll take a look, over."

"Roger that." The radio fell silent.

Denzel pointed to the jetty and stepped from the tree line. There was no haste in his movement, just the fast low approach of a man ready for anything.

Lynn followed suit, avoiding the icy water as they crossed the grey rocks lining the shore. "See anything?"

"Not—" he raised a stalling hand. "Hear that?"

Lynn hadn't, until a whip crack broke the silence. "I heard that. Rifle?"

"Definitely!" Denzel increased his pace, flattening himself against the kiosk wall.

Lynn arrived a second later, her heart mimicking a pounding sledgehammer. "They … shoot at … us?"

"No, there was no bullet impact near us."

Denzel eased around the building to the jetty side. If he was scared, he showed no evidence as he surveyed the other buildings.

Lynn felt a tremble as she crouched behind him. She looked toward the water and gasped.

"Oh no, we got blood on the Jetty."

The stark redness almost glowed against the white-painted boards.

"Shit, I hope we're not too late."

Denzel tried the kiosk door without taking his eyes from the boat shed. It creaked open allowing him to glance inside.

"Okay, you hide in here. Call Erica and get the police here fast."

"What about you?"

"I need to see what's happening. I'll help Bruce if I can."

"Then I'm …"

"No, you're staying here. You don't need to risk your life today." Denzel's voice was firm but not unkind.

"And you do?"

He shook his head. "You have a husband and son waiting for you. Nobody's telling them you got shot dead on my watch. I'm alone, if I die it doesn't matter."

Lynn blinked back tears. "Wrong! It matters to me. You matter to me." She squeezed his arm. "How are you getting to the boat shed?"

"I'm going around the gift shop into the trees. I can creep around the rear from there." He took her wrist. "Please, hide in there."

Lynn pressed the emergency beacon on her radio. "Let's go."

Before he could stop her, she dashed across the gravel path and gained the cover of the gift shop. Little boats, compasses, bookmarks and T-shirts could be seen through the window. The smell of bait oozed from the wooden structure.

"Damn it!" Denzel grumbled as he stepped onto the path.

"Going somewhere?" asked a cold voice amid the clacking of a bolt action rifle.

"Sure," Denzel raised his arms. "I was going to the gift shop."

"It closed days ago." said the man, sneering over the sights of his weapon. His faded ginger moustache and hair were slicked with sweat despite the cold.

"Pity, I was going to buy an oar to break over your head."

Lynn hid a chuckle; Denzel always had a way with words. She slipped behind the gift shop.

"Ha! Funny, arsehole," He pointed behind him. "Where's the other one? I know there were two of you."

"We heard your gunshot. She headed for our truck on White Peak Road to get help."

"Ha! She abandoned you?"

"No, I'm a gentleman I sent her to get help, so she'd be safe."

"If you lied about her, I'll…"

"Yeah, yeah. Shoot and feed me to the bears, I know."

"Shut up and walk to the boat shed or die where you stand. Move!"

"Why are you here?" Denzel walked past him keeping his pace levelled and slow.

"The boss has …"

Lynn heard no more as the men walked from earshot. She angled into the trees as Denzel planned. She watched her partner stroll across the car park as if enjoying an evening walk.

"How'd you do it, Denz? I'd be a shaking wreck under that gun."

She updated Erica on the radio. Against her better judgement, she edged around the car park until she was at the boat shed.

"There's always a bleedin' hero," said a second man inside, his voice deep and aggressive. "Why didn't you kill 'im on sight, Willard?"

"There was a woman. He said she went for help. Thought we might need this one as a hostage if she tries anything."

"I see. Get out there and find 'er. Both of you."

Lynn tensed. That meant she was dealing with three men now. Two goons and their leader. She slipped into the shadows of a bush bearing furry catkins. A woolly willow that was becoming scarce these days.

"Check the jetty and buildings. The bloke looked in the Kiosk. I'll see if I can find her trail and prove she went for their truck."

"You must be Willard," Lynn breathed whilst watching the two split and begin their search. She needed a plan. She was also wearing bright orange, a bad idea, she'd be caught soon.

"Where are you, lady?" Willard called as he disappeared along the front of the boatshed. His boots crunched on the frost.

'Yellowjacket.' Lynn remembered the case of young Angie and her father Gus. They'd left his jacket to mark their trail that day. Face set with determination, she parted the willow and made her move.

"Gotcha!" Willard remarked minutes later, his attention upon a bright orange rescue jacket hiding in the bushes. "Get out here!"

Lynn froze, holding her breath.

"I said, get out here!" Willard raised his gun and approached. "What the hell?!"

The rescue jacket was being worn by a sapling spruce tree, its arms spread by deadfall branches.

"Hi!" Lynn made her voice cheery.

Willard flinched and spun fast.

A hefty branch slammed into his stomach, driving the air from his lungs.

Lynn watched him drop his gun and double over. She rotated her weapon cracking it hard against his exposed jaw.

Willard snapped backwards and lay groaning through at least two broken teeth.

"Now, whose got who?" she said calmer than she felt. Her hands trembled around the branch as she took a step toward the boat shed and froze.

"One more step and I'll blow your brains out." The second man had his rifle sight aimed right at her head.

"Kill her!" Willard mumbled as he made it to his knees.

"Nobody needs to die to —" Lynn dropped.

Blam! The rifle's retort echoed across the lake scattering birds.

The bullet removed hairs from Lynn's head. She hit the deck feeling nothing but relief for a second.

Willard yelped, his body trembled as it lost motor functions and then flopped to the ground.

Lynn fought with the urge to vomit, he'd been hit above the ear, blowing apart his skull.

"Oh, shit! Oh, shit!" The other man staggered about shocked and panicked by his actions.

"What's your name?" Lynn rose to her feet with her hands raised.

"J-Joey."

"Okay, Joey. I need you to put the gun down, for me."

Something crashed inside the boat shed.

"If that was Lynn getting shot. You're a dead man!" Denzel yelled.

"I'm d-dead too." Joey looked at his rifle.

"Not if you put the weapon down. Do that for me now," Lynn urged in a soft voice. "I promise you'll…"

Hell was breaking loose in the shed. Something shattered, then a yell of pain followed by a feminine scream. Another bang and running footsteps reached through the wooden walls.

Joey seemed glued to his gun as thoughts ran through his mind. Then coming to a decision, he looked at Lynn. "I gotta kill yer, coz I can't go to prison."

"No, Joey. You don't —"

He chambered another bullet, raised the rifle and stepped forward to aim at her.

"She's dead and so are you!" said a man inside the boatshed.

"Joey, stop!" Lynn pressed a palm toward him, begging. Tears burned her eyes as she saw images of her husband and son. She was due to eat at the pub with them tonight to celebrate her son's eighth birthday.

"I'm sorry. I gotta." He depressed the trigger.

A male roar preceded a monumental thud. The wooden wall shattered as if hit by a grenade. Denzel flew out like a charging rhino taking his captor with him.

Both slammed into Joey, his gun bucked as he tumbled to the frozen ground. The shot whizzed over Lynn's head and vanished into the forest.

Denzel rose bleeding and furious. He grabbed Joey's gun and blasted him across the head with the stock.

The man went limp.

"You ruined everything!" said the leader rising like an embattled drunk.

"No, Ludwig. You did. Bruce told you this place was not for sale. You tried to steal it. Your greed caused this mess," Denzel retorted as the rage melted from his face on seeing Lynn alive. "Good to see you," he said.

"You too," Lynn half-smiled.

Ludwig had noticed Willard's body. His face contorted with rage, his eyes like a demon's as he looked toward Lynn. "You killed him! You killed my son!"

"No, it was an accident. Joey tried to kill me and missed," she said backing away from him. "Please, calm —"

He roared and lunged.

Denzel seized his coat, hauled him around and cracked him with a meaty punch.

Despite a broken nose, Ludwig swung wildly for him.

Denzel hit him again.

He staggered toward Lynn.

She ducked a flailing fist and landed a punch of her own, square on his jaw.

This time his eyes rolled, and he collapsed to the ground.

"Lynn, are you okay?" Denzel asked hugging her.

"I hate violence," she replied in a shaky voice. "Are Bruce and his family okay?"

"Me too," Denzel took a bandana from his pocket to wipe blood from his face. "They're inside. They'll need medical help but will be fine."

"What the hell happened?" Police Detective Howlett demanded to know an hour later. The car park was filled with police vehicles, ambulances and a rescue truck by then.

"Ludwig believed this land was his. He tried to buy the place and business for a paltry sum. When Bruce refused,

Ludwig abducted his family and tried to force him to sell." Denzel explained while a paramedic patched his wounds.

"So, you broke his face?" Howlett said, watching Ludwig getting wheeled into an ambulance, still unconscious and handcuffed.

"He tried to kill Lynn and I for interfering. Left us no choice but to defend ourselves." Denzel shrugged.

"I see, excuse me."

Denzel walked along the Jetty. Lynn was standing by the water. "You okay?"

"That was a close one. I nearly died because I didn't listen to you."

"Had you listened Joey would have found and shot you in the kiosk. You did very well today."

"Maybe, Willard's dead though. We still have to get those boats back too."

"It was his and Joey's fault for going along with their dad's crazed ways."

"I agree, I'll get my jet ski and fetch the hire boats," said Bruce, approaching. A portly man, he looked friendly even with a black eye and busted lip. "I want to thank you for saving my family."

"Any time," Denzel shook his hand. "I take it you released the boats onto the lake?"

"Yes, he clobbered me the day we closed for winter. I managed to set the boats free that night. I knew someone would spot them and come to see what happened."

"You were right," Lynn smiled. "The signal for help can take many forms. It's important to read the signs and take action when help is required."

THE BANDANA BOND

By Betty Mermelstein

You could say a washtub brought them together. Not very romantic, but the heart can make itself known through many means. The day was a scorcher: the kind that kept you swallowing for any drop of moisture to slide down your throat. The hired hands had been out riding fences to see if a break had occurred anywhere. The cattle were too valuable to the ranch to let any escape, no matter how much the weather put a cowboy into a sweat.

Janet had been in the yard bent over a giant tub of water with dwindling suds. She didn't mind the heat, as long as she could dip her hands again and again into the cool water and perform her task under the shade of the cottonwood. She was nearly done when she heard the men riding back toward the house for their midday meal.

Their horses seemed to dip their heads even lower than usual, plodding with their last steps toward the welcome water trough. The cowboys were as intent as their animals but managed to tip their hats as they passed by Janet. One of them stopped in front of her.

"I'd give up the last few yards and let my horse drink from that tub if I didn't think he'd get the hiccups from those bubbles," the cowboy named Ben joked.

Janet looked up at him, taking her hands from the water and wiping them on her apron.

"You can go right ahead and see," she laughed. "My Grandpa's Long Johns in there won't mind!"

Ben shared the laugh and wiped his face with his bandana, wiping away the sweat and grime that caused his face to glisten. Janet couldn't help but notice how much dirt was indeed upon that bandana after a hard morning's work.

"I would offer to drop that bandana there in my tub and give it a good wash. It will dry somewhat while you're eating and keep you cool this afternoon."

Ben immediately untied the bandana from his neck and handed it over to Janet. As she took it, she noticed the geometric arrangement of repeated squares with a composition of arrow-shaped designs.

"That's a nice one," she said, dropping it into the thinning suds.

Ben tipped his hat to her and rode on to meet up with the others. An hour later he sported a damp neckerchief and a smile on his face.

Janet had long finished her washing when the sun spread its shades of red low in the sky. She stood on the porch watching the evening scene when one of the hired hands came galloping toward the house, stopping long enough to throw himself off his horse and tie it loosely to the porch railing. He continued at a run into the house. Within a minute, Janet's father and brothers exploded from the front door and ran for their own horses.

"What's wrong?" she shouted after them.

"A mountain lion spooked Ben's horse and threw him to the ground," one of her brothers managed to say before he disappeared from sight.

Not Ben, Janet thought. Not the one whom she had watched for months, smiled at when he passed by, and relished any conversation that passed between them.

She spent the next hour pacing on the porch, kicking at any stray stones that got in her way, and scrutinizing the horizon for any dark forms that would be heading homeward. Finally, she saw them: all the cowboys riding, but not with urgency, she noticed. The shapes were upright on their horses, except one. That one was horizontal and flopped with each stride of the animal.

When the group reached the house, Janet stepped toward the men next to where Ben lay face down in his saddle. Everyone stopped, allowing her to approach his body as if they knew she had a special need to be near him one more time. There, freely dangling from Ben's neck, was his bandana that had been untied after he had fallen and hit his head. Janet clasped the end of it and pulled so that it slipped from him, completing a physical connection that would be the only one between the two.

Janet balled up the fabric and squeezed it in her hand, then unfurled it and hooked it over the waistband of her skirt. She knew it would be placed there every day: a symbol of an irretrievable love.

GOLDEN GIRL
By Pamela Smith

A row of lightbulbs illuminate the bathroom, the mirror below them reflecting my exhausted features back at me. The walls are a gorgeous light blue, and the deep sink is surrounded by a white marble countertop, ready to catch my falling hair as I cut it. A gold faucet matches the gold handle on the toilet - installing them was a pain in the ass for my father.

Just as I'm brushing my hair out one last time, there is a sudden, loud banging on the bathroom door. I jump, dropping the scissors I'd been holding. Placing a hand over my racing heart, I glance in the direction of the door.

My father's voice, filled with anxiety, yells through it. "Gold Rush!"

No more words need to be said. Rushing to the door, I fling it open and nearly collide with my father. We've had close calls - lesser alerts caused by those who were greedy or overly curious. But never a Gold Rush. We knew it would happen eventually, but the shock that it's real and not one of our regular drills sends a shiver down my spine.

As I stumble a step back, so as not to run into him, his gloved hands - gloves that are so long they reach his elbows - grip my shoulders. "You know what you need to do. I love you."

Tears fill his eyes, and they bring to mind the deep blue oceans I've read about. Though I too want to cry, I force myself to stay strong. As much for me as for him. I glance towards his hair. He tries to keep it short, yet it grows so quickly he's hardly able to keep up with it. His hair resembles a realistic metallic gold. But of course it would - it *is* real. Forcing myself to refocus, I quickly hug him and rush into my room.

I yank a hat onto my head, shoving my hair underneath it as best I can. I really wish I'd been able to finish cutting it. Grabbing my bag from under the bed - a bag I've had prepared for years - I walk over to the window and pull the curtain slightly open, chancing a look outside. A mob approaches my home, carrying the stereotypical pitch forks, torches, and shovels — I've never understood the purpose of the shovels — with the occasional bow and arrow thrown in for good measure.

Closing the curtain and turning away, I'm faced with the darkness of my room. A single bright lantern sits in the corner. The shadows from the furniture seem as if they're stretching towards me, ready to trap me. The small size of the room becomes suffocating, and I realize I can't stay here any longer.

I quickly give my father one last hug, then run out the bedroom door and down the stairs. I just barely make it out the back door when I hear the front one bust off its hinges.

Dark clouds cover the even darker sky above me, deep gray and threatening. Thick humidity surrounds me, making it harder to breathe. I've nearly crossed the territory line - we'd always lived close to the edge of town, just in case - when it starts raining. It's not a light drizzle, but a heavy downpour. The rain is cold – a strong fall breeze blows it nearly sideways. Running straight into the wind does not make my effort any easier, but I'm not about to give up. I'm the only option left to save my father. But first, I need to find safety.

My father isn't a man of many words. He enjoys my company but otherwise prefers to keep a low profile. However, Father is easily distinguishable in a crowd – too distinguishable. His hair and gloves are a dead giveaway – but it's not like he can hide who he is. When you work for the King, you can only stay out of the spotlight for so long. The legends of my father have spread throughout the world, transcending culture, languages, and time. Money, particularly gold, is universal. But legends lie. They've got his status wrong, his name wrong, his family wrong. We don't live in Greece, and we really don't know anything about Greek gods. The only thing they've got right is his touch.

See, Father's not a king, the name Midas means nothing, we aren't rich, and he is the most humble person I know, completely indifferent to what he could benefit from as a result of his…well, I wouldn't call it a gift. And I don't think he would either. His name is Mark, born to simple parents living on a farm in the middle of nowhere. He found a wife just as humble as he, though my mother died years ago.

The only gold things in our home were things he couldn't manage to handle with gloves on. He had me. His life isn't one of extravagance.

The only thing Father wasn't prepared for was my hair. Thick strands of gold hair streaking through platinum blonde. Hence, the need to cut it regularly. It wasn't perfect. If someone looked close enough, they'd see the metallic contrast with the rest of the hair. But that was why I escaped the minute danger crossed our door. The King had offered my father protection, a home in the castle, but he refused. And then guards instead, which he also refused. He wanted as little to do with that lifestyle as possible.

But Father's work for the King is part of the reason for our danger. Not a choice, the role was forced upon him because of his parents' debt. When the King asks for gold, the gloves come off and gold is given. He's turned even a chicken into gold. The problem is, rather than share the wealth, the King has a nasty habit of abusing his financial power and leaving the town poor and its citizens desperate. It's so severe that there was no advancement within the towns and villages, including when it comes to weapons. It left the citizens nearly defenseless. They won't harm Father, he's too valuable. But he was adamant that I escape rather than be taken as well.

I can touch anything. They'll stay in whatever form their atomic molecules originally designed them to be. But my hair is indispensable. As quickly as you cut the strands, they grow back at the same rate. It's basically an unending flow of money, and people are greedy and selfish. Even so, I've left the house to go into town for supplies or whatnot. My hair is just usually really short.

My thoughts are interrupted when I'm forced to stop right at the edge of town. I'm soaked to the bone, my teeth are chattering, and I'm shivering periodically. We had an escape plan and, although I never knew exactly why, it was always to go through the forest and get to the next town. However, right now, a large tree lay across the path in front of me. Walking around would take too long, so my only option is to climb.

I glance back with just enough time to see someone point in my direction. A groan escapes my lips as I realize I've been spotted. Even through the storm, I can hear how close they're getting. I quickly climb up and over the tree, landing on the other side just as I hear an arrow strike the tree. My heart races as I take off running again, adrenaline providing me with another burst of energy. Branches break as I barrel through bushes, others crunch underneath my feet. I intend to follow my father's instruction and the escape plan through its entirety.

I walk along the edge of the road, close to the stores, in the hope of avoiding anyone's prying eyes. I'm careful to stay out of crowds and take alleys whenever I can or need to. The sky is dark, and the stars are both beautiful and unnerving. Nature shouldn't be allowed to shine so bright when my emotions are so faded. Though the dark does make it much easier to hide.

By the time I reach the edge of this town - of which I don't even know the name - the moon is at its zenith. I shift my backpack to my shoulder and make my way into yet another forest ahead of me. My mind is groggy, and my eyes struggle to focus due to exhaustion, but I try to stay alert, even as I know I'm barely covering my tracks.

I crawl through the broken window of an abandoned cabin, trying to avoid getting cut by the glass and just barely succeeding. As I jump onto the floor, I explore my new hideout, content to find a bed. Checking the dusty dresser drawers, I sigh in relief when I find clothes. They smell stale, but I change anyway. Anything to get out of these sopping wet clumps of fabric that really no longer do anything but keep me cold.

I collapse onto the bed backwards, ignoring the dust that puffs up around me, and stare at the fan above me – a fan caked with just as much dust as the bed. I lay there for an hour, listening intently to make sure I'm safe, and eventually fall asleep, my body too worn out to stay awake any longer.

I'm packing my bag with other stolen clothes,

preparing to leave, when I hear the sound of banging on the door. There are people banging on an abandoned building in the middle of a forest. There's no way they just stumbled upon it and decided to get aggressive.

My hat fell off at some point during my nap and my hair flows freely down my back. The longer my hair, the easier it is to see the golden streaks, and right now, they are clearly visible.

The door crashes open and I jump, grabbing the hat and attempting to stuff my hair back underneath it as I do. I fail miserably in my haste, the hat slipping back off my head instead.

"I know you're here! You thought you could hide, but you're not that sneaky. Too many little clues. Pathetic." It's a man's voice. He chuckles darkly. "You better come out willingly. Unless you want to do this the hard way."

The voice of the stranger is a growl, the venom in his voice obvious. He sounds like he'd really like to do this the hard way. I hear something scrape along the wooden walls.

I glance around the room fervently, desperate to find a way out, the window too high to climb back through. When I can't find a way, I frantically start searching through drawers and underneath furniture, trying to find something to defend myself with. The dust becomes a cloud around me and I loudly sneeze.

The door to the room slams open a moment later, and two men enter, at least double my size. I back up to the wall behind me as they approach closer, trying to remember all of my training – mainly hand-to-hand combat, but also shooting a bow and arrow or sword work. Father had insisted upon me learning ways to defend myself should I need to.

"All we want is that beautiful hair…though we would need to take you with us. Considering hair does grow back." The first man says, his deep brown eyes glinting mischievously as he scratches at his beard with the tip of a knife. I watch wearily, surprised he isn't cutting himself.

"Don't worry, we'd take good care of you. Wouldn't we, Ryan?" The man continues casually, as if kidnapping – or, rather, teen-napping – is an occurrence that can just be brushed off.

"Of course, Ethan." The second man – apparently named Ryan – replies.

I start shaking, my eyes desperately searching the room once again. My bag lays on the floor by the bed. If I even can get away, I'll have to leave it. The idea fills me with sadness. It's all I have left to remind me of home.

A third voice suddenly joins the other two.

"Leave her alone." Followed by an unfamiliar click.

Ryan laughs manically, glancing behind him, and sneers at the sight of the young man standing there. "And what do you think you're going to do?"

"Shoot you." The young guy's voice is calm, and his gaze never falters as he stares back at the man before him. I'm too distracted trying to figure out what the guy means by 'shoot him' to even pay attention to the other two.

Ryan raises a short mace, which I hadn't even noticed,

and attempts to attack, though it is easily dodged as the young guy ducks, simultaneously adjusting his...whatever that is. Suddenly, there's a quick and loud bang, and Ryan falls to the ground, screaming in pain. I flinch, my ears ringing for a moment.

The first man - Ethan - turns around, though he doesn't attack. The young man doesn't bother to wait for him to speak. He tackles Ethan, rushing him into the bed's corner post. As the man's back hits it, his head flies back as well, knocking against the post, and he falls to the floor.

"We need to go." The young man says as he stands and brushes some dust off his clothes, his voice still calm despite what just occurred.

He grabs my bag, motioning for me to follow him. Without waiting for my reply, he walks out the door.

I hesitate, realize the men are starting to recollect themselves and that this guy has my bag, and quickly follow after him. I rush to fall into step beside him, both annoyed at his nonchalant attitude and grateful for his help.

He makes his way into the forest I'd left the night before, walking back the way I'd come. I'm starting to get tired of trees. The morning sun nearly blinds me, the trees providing little to no coverage.

"Who are you? Why did you help me?" I glance at the L-shaped thing – a weapon? – in his hand. "And what is that?"

"Call me Spence. This is a gun." He ignores the second question; eyes trained on the path in front of us. He barely acknowledges me, and it's almost as if he's on high alert for any other dangers.

I glance back to see if we're being followed and, seeing we're safe for the moment, I continue pressing him for answers.

"How did you find me? Why did you save me?"

He stops, sighs, and turns to look at me with narrowed eyes and an expression that's clearly exasperation.

"Look, I saw the guys banging on the door when I walked by. Heard what they said. Didn't seem like a good situation." He turns away and continues walking. I rush to catch up. His short answers bug me.

"Well, thanks. But can I have my bag? I kinda need to go."

He ignores the question and side-eyes me, making me uncomfortable. "No. I'll be traveling with you."

I stop and stare at his back as he continues walking. "What gives you the right–"

"Just shut up." I'm too shocked by his harshness to keep arguing and instead continue to follow him.

Spence stays by my side, never giving up the bag.

"So, what's the plan?" He asks later that afternoon as we eat sausages he'd stolen from a nearby village and cooked over a fire. The sun shines brightly, occasionally blocked by a stray cloud, and a strong wind causes tree branches to sway.

"What are you talking about?" Something about the way he'd asked the question makes me feel as if he's not talking about where we are going or how we're going to avoid those goons we'd left behind.

He cautiously glances around us and is just about to respond when a loud rustling in the bushes nearby interrupts him. A moment later, an arrow flies into a tree trunk just behind Spence, narrowly avoiding his head.

Without hesitation, he jumps up, grabs my bag, runs over to me, and yanks me up by the arm.

Dragging me along, he runs in the opposite direction.

I can hear the impact of feet on grass as we're pursued. We duck as we run, making ourselves as small a target as possible.

"Get back here!" I recognize the voice as one of the men we'd escaped from, though I'm not sure if it's Ethan or Ryan. Another arrow, and another tree trunk is impacted.

Spence nearly throws me into a large group of bushes, tosses my bag on top of me, and hisses "Stay here" in my direction.

I cower deeper into the bushes, clutching my bag as if it's a lifeline, and listen carefully for signs of fighting.

I watch as Spence suddenly runs past the bushes, not even glancing in my direction. Ethan and Ryan run after him, the knife and mace glinting in the sunlight. My mouth goes dry, and I begin to shake at the sound of the gun again.

After what feels like forever, I hear steps coming towards the bushes. I squeeze the bag tighter, my heart pounding in my chest. Spence's head peaks over the bush in front of me and I sigh in relief. His eyebrow is cut, blood flowing down over his eye. He seems to not even notice.

He holds his hand out in my direction and, after I grab it, pulls me out of the bushes. "Are you okay?"

I ignore his question. "Are you?"

I eye his torn clothes and the wound on his arm. He just nods in response and begins walking. I follow.

We pass by the bodies of the two men, and I silently

wonder if they're dead or just passed out.

Somehow, I feel like it's the former.

After a few minutes, I stop abruptly and grab his arm to stop him as well.

"What's going on?" My voice is surprisingly calm.

He looks at me, realizes I won't let him avoid questions any longer, and sighs before answering.

"I know who you are." He runs his fingers through his hair. "Your father and the King put together a plan a long time ago for your protection, should something happen."

I blink in surprise, staring at him in shock and at a loss for words. The wind whips my hair around me and the gold strands shine in the sun.

"I wasn't supposed to be seen. But you have a tendency to get into trouble," he continues slowly, glancing at my hair momentarily before shifting his eyes to my face, watching for a reaction.

"Wait…where's my father?" I say this more harshly

than I'd intended as it occurs to me he may know.

He hesitates long enough for me to know that he does.

"Where is my father?" My voice takes a hard edge as I step toward him, glaring up at his face.

I'm sure I don't look nearly as threatening as I feel.

He sighs once more, heavier this time, and runs his fingers through his hair again.

"He's locked away in some house in another town. The King has been preparing a rescue mission, but it takes time."

Without another word, I turn away from him and head toward the castle. Having had no knowledge of where my father could have been, I hadn't quite thought out how to rescue him yet. Too busy trying to, well, live. But now, I'll be damned if I don't join that rescue mission. He grabs my arm and stops me this time.

"Don't even think about it."

I yank my arm from his grasp and keep walking. I'm only a few steps away before I hear him following me. He's not going to stop me, not this time.

The wind howls, thunder growing ever closer. Lighting strikes occasionally, lighting up the ground beneath it. Rain pelts me hard and heavy. I'm drenched in seconds. This is becoming repetitive. I try to ignore it, eyeing the King's castle. I watch from behind a tree as a soldier paces in front of the bridge leading to the entrance. I can hear Spence mumbling to himself in annoyance.

"I don't like this."

"I don't care." My eyes don't leave my target and my voice is hard.

"This is dangerous.

"For *you*." I echo my first response.

I hear him groan from beside me. "I'm well aware."

A moment later, I see my chance. The soldier glances at the castle, not long, but long enough. I sneak behind him;

hearing Spence follow me.

"I'm worried about you. Just let me—" Spence starts to say as we move.

"No," I interrupt him quickly.

The wind picks up, blowing my hair everywhere and causing intense knots. I attempt to sneak past the guard, only to find myself unsuccessful.

Lightning strikes once more, showing my face. The soldier sees me, reaching for what looks like another gun thing, but Spence steps up beside me and, to my surprise, the soldier immediately relaxes. Before he can speak, I do.

"Where's my father?"

"This is too dangerous for you. You need to go. We'll rescue him." His voice sounds desperate.

Spence doesn't move, staying silent. We wait him out, and eventually he speaks.

The soldier narrows his eyes, clearly frustrated. "He's in Boulder." He names a town nearby. "There're too many people. You won't be able to get him on your own."

I don't say anything for a moment, but slowly it dawns on me that he's right. I'm more likely to get captured myself than save my father.

"Then take me to the King." I hear Spencer let out a small sigh of relief.

The King sits upon his throne, turned into gold by my father. The room around him is much larger than necessary. Deep red banners line the walls, coinciding perfectly with pure white pillars that are wrapped in a gold vine-like design.

He talks with a soldier beside him, his mannerisms portraying his focus on the task at hand. He looks up as the soldier from the bridge, me, and Spence enter the room.

"I thought I told you to stay hidden Spencer."

He narrows his eyes at my companion. He doesn't ask who I am, though I assume he doesn't have to.

Spencer rolls his eyes. "With her, it's impossible. She draws too much attention." I stare at Spence in shock, unable to believe how casually he is speaking to our King.

With a sigh, the King turns to me. "I can't say I'm surprised. I'm assuming you want to know about your father," he states more than asks.

"Yes, Your Highness. I want to take part in his rescue."

The King shakes his head. "That is out of the question. Your father is dear to me, and he requested your safety. I intend to keep my promise."

I internally question whether my father is 'dear to him' due to his ability or as a friend.

I force myself to remain calm, though I internally scream. Spence replies before I can.

"She won't take no for an answer, trust me." He folds his arms as he glances at me, a look of both annoyance and concern on his face, before turning back to the King.

The King stares at Spence, seemingly searching his face for...something. I couldn't even begin to guess what. Finally, the King nods once.

"Very well. But you are to go with her. Stay by her side." He nods to the soldier beside us, who leaves, returning to the entrance.

The soldier who was beside the King approaches us. "My name is Dylan. I will be leading the rescue. I'll escort you to a room. We aren't attempting the rescue until tomorrow night."

"Wouldn't tonight's storm help hide us though?" I was anxious to get going, even if it had to be through a thunderstorm.

Dylan appraises me. "You're smart," he says this very matter-of-factly, a slight grin on his face. "Yes, that would work to our advantage. But we aren't quite yet prepared. We have a few more supply runs to make tomorrow before we're entirely ready. Besides, it would be good for you to spend tomorrow learning at least basic self-defense. I'll pair you with a soldier—"

Spence interrupts. "I will teach her."

I frown and jump in. "I already know enough."

They share a look, then glance at me quizzically. I sigh. "Father taught me enough to defend myself, if need be, but the plan was always to escape first."

Dylan looks at him, then me, and nods. "Understood. If you would follow me." He begins walking towards a door in the far corner.

I look towards Spence. "Are you coming?" The nerves hit at the idea of leaving Spencer.

He smirks and shakes his head. "I have a room already. Go rest, I'll meet with you tomorrow after breakfast. I'm at least teaching you to use a gun." He turns and walks away.

I rush towards Dylan, who is waiting for me at the door. He holds it open as I walk through, then enters after me and closes it. Moving in front of me, he leads me down one hall after another. It doesn't take long for me to become completely disoriented. There is no way I could navigate these halls on my own.

"Hey Dylan, why is Spence so casual with the King?" My question seems to surprise him and his step falters for a second.

"That is something you will have to talk to him about." I frown, unhappy with the answer.

He stops in front of a random door and motions towards the room behind it.

"You will stay here. Someone will come to collect you for breakfast in the morning. I suggest you be prepared."

He walks off before I can say anything - which includes a question of just when I should be ready.

Shaking my head, I step inside and spend the remainder of my night mentally preparing for the events of tomorrow.

After breakfast the next day, I meet with Spence, who makes sure I review the basics of hand-to-hand combat and swordsmanship – to make sure I really do know what I'm doing – but he also teaches me to shoot a gun. Thankfully, I'm relatively fit from my training at home, so the exercise doesn't exhaust me as much as he probably expected.

He steps forward once we're finished and gently grabs hold of the ends of a few strands of my hair, which instantly makes me blush.

"You should cut this. We have an in-house hairdresser."

My eyes narrow at the word 'we' but I decide against trying to figure that out right now. I need to stay focused on my father's rescue. He lets go of my hair and it falls over my shoulder. The gold glints in the sunlight.

"It will help hide you. Keep you safer," he says, interrupting my thoughts.

"Fine," I mumble, barely making the word audible, and he chuckles, leading me away toward my hair's demise.

We approach the town in which my father is trapped. A line of soldiers stretches out on either side of Spence and I, kneeling behind trees or bushes and watching for a prime opportunity to invade. The wind howls, echoing off the mountains surrounding the town. My hair, now a short pixie cut, is hidden beneath a solid gold – yet somehow still light – helmet, matching the armor I'd been given.

Suddenly, a loud yell sounds at the end of the line and soldier after soldier echoes it, like a wave's rough, rumbling crescendo. Without looking at me, Spence says that it's time, and we take off towards the town.

As Spence and I run through the fight, I narrowly avoid slashes and stabs. They've literally brought swords to a gun fight, not that they had a choice. I doubt most of these townsfolk even know what a gun is. I didn't, and my father actually works for the King. Spence fights beside me, simultaneously protecting me and felling anyone who gets in his way.

The howls of the wind merge with the clash of swords, gunshots, and screams of victory, pain, or both. The town has become a battlefield. Getting to the home is much easier than expected, almost too easy. Dylan had ordered the soldiers to distract - and 'decommission' - any townsperson that tried to stop us, resulting in a clear path. Though why he'd focus solely on protecting us is beyond me. There's no way my father is that important.

Once inside the home, Spence makes quick work of disarming the two townspeople guarding the basement. I shove my way past him and barrel into the door, not even considering the fact that it could be locked.

With a loud thump, I'm bounced back and hit the floor. The armor prevents any substantial injuries, but there was still a slight aching in my head – I could tell that later it would become worse, likely a headache, adrenaline was just keeping the pain at bay.

Spencer curses under his breath at my impulsiveness, makes sure I'm okay, then kneels down and skillfully picks the lock. We run down to the basement. It's clear it's never used. Through a window, I can see the light of day has begun fading, the dark providing both trouble and cover. In the center of the room is my father, blindfolded, hands tied behind his back and degloved. Miscellaneous gold figurines occupy the ground around him.

We quickly free him, being careful to make sure we re-glove him first, and make our way back out of the house. The ground is littered with dead bodies, injured men, and weapons, blood soaks the ground beneath them, making the dirt an even darker brown than it already is. I look away, struggling against the queasy feeling in my stomach.

I sit with my father in the guest room of the castle, exhausted, but happy he's alive. Father sleeps peacefully in his bed as I hold his hand in mine. A soft knock on the door arouses me from my persistent nodding off.

"Come in."

Spence enters the room and gestures to a chair as a

request to sit. I nod. He pulls the chair next to me and smiles. "I'm glad he's okay."

I smile gratefully and glance at him in curiosity. "So why you?"

His eyes narrow in confusion. "Huh?"

"To protect me," I explain.

His eyes get a mischievous, playful gleam, something I haven't seen from him before. "Simple."

He grins and reaches over to brush some hair from my eyes. His touch lingers for a second longer than necessary. I feel my face flush as a blush creeps onto my cheeks again.

"I'll tell you a secret," he pauses to lean in and whisper in my ear, causing me to blush harder.

"I'm the King's hidden son."

QUACKS

By Robert Mackey

"Harvey...Harvey...HARVEY!"

Harvey mumbled to himself. "Damnit, woman."

He screamed over his shoulder toward the living room, "WHAT?!"

Agnes waddled into the kitchen. "The people at NASA said there's now ten meteors. Nine more just seemed to appear out of nowhere and one is going to hit right here in Littleton in the next fifteen minutes or so! They say they're as big as houses!"

Harvey tonged ears of corn out of a pot, placing them in a big bowl, unresponsive.

Agnes, arms waving over her head, cried, "Well, aren't you going to do something?"

"What would you have me do?"

Completing her third lap around the kitchen table, arms still waving overhead, she yelled, "Grab the dog! Get some clothes! Get in the car! Get out of here!

"If a house-sized meteor lands within fifty miles of us, we're toast. If there's ten of 'em, trust me, it's the end of the world."

Agnes stopped. "So, you're just going to eat corn?"

"Yup. If you want some, I'll be on the deck. May as well have a front row seat."

"Shouldn't we hide in the basement?"

"If a meteor that big hits here we won't have a basement."

"What do you mean if? The people at NASA said…"

"The people at NASA are a bunch of quacks."

Harvey calmly opened the patio slider. Placing his bowl of butter smothered corn on the patio table, he sat down. Agnes paced back and forth nervously watching the sky.

Harvey picked up an ear, smiled at the dripping butter, leaned forward, and before he could sink his teeth into the juicy, yellow kernels, a gigantic egg landed in the middle of the high school football field right behind Harvey and Agnes's house with a thud. Agnes fell silent for the first time in years.

"I told you they're quacks. Can't even tell an egg from a meteor."

A thundering crack rattled the windows of the house. The halves of the shell shot out in opposite directions. Harvey and Agnes looked up nearly falling backward as the head of a duck rose skyward. The duck stood, shook its head and tail furiously. Looking down at the couple, it emitted a singular quack.

Agnes's head slowly tuned toward Harvey. Her eyes remained on the spectacle taking up the entire football field.

"It's a giant duck!"

"Nothing gets by you, Agnes," said Harvey, through a mouthful of corn.

"It's got an extremely skinny neck for a duck that size," said Agnes.

Reaching over the chain link fence, the duck snapped up Agnes, threw its head back and swallowed Agnes whole.

Harvey said, pointing at the duck with an ear of corn, "Thank you for that. Would you like to wash her down with some juicy, sweet corn?"

The duck reached down and delicately took the corn from Harvey's outstretched hand.

Mrs. Ornstein, one of Harvey's least favorite neighbors, rounded the corner of the house into Harvey's back yard.

"Oh my! That's one big duck! It has an awfully ski ..."

"Don't tell it it has a ..."

The duck reached down and plucked the woman from the lawn, sending her to join Agnes.

"... skinny neck."

Harvey smiled up at the duck. "Wow my friend, you're batting a thousand."

Harvey placed his bowl of corn out on the lawn. "I'll be right back."

Harvey darted into the garage, grabbed a thousand-foot roll of construction grade string line, a Stanley knife, and his compound bow.

Harvey stepped out on the deck, asking the duck, "You mind if I put a string around your most regal neck?"

The duck quacked.

"I'll take that as a yes."

Harvey unraveled a couple hundred feet of string, tied one end to an arrow and the other end to his index finger. He shot the arrow straight up into the air. The arrow reached the end of its tether and fell to earth just on the other side of the duck's head as it plucked another ear of corn from the bowl. Harvey ducked under the ducks' outstretched neck, slipped the string off his finger, made a loop on both ends, poked one end through the other, tying the free end to his wrist. The duck lifted its head cinching the string around its neck.

Harvey smiled, nodding his satisfaction at how things were going.

"Heel, Timothy. You don't mind if I call you Timothy, do you?"

The duck let out another quack.

"Well, shall we go find your friends?"

Another quack.

Harvey headed around the side of his house. The duck took a shortcut, flattening Harvey's house as he followed. Harvey looked up at Timothy.

"You couldn't have used the neighbor's house as a walkway?"

Timothy cocked his head to one side as a response.

"No matter."

People lined the sidewalks conversing about the loud thud, the crack, the giant duck they saw over Harvey's place which was now being led down the street by Harvey himself. Harvey walked by, eyes forward, not acknowledging one of them. He stopped in front of one of his neighbor's houses, one whose yard was home to several defunct vehicles and weeds and grass nearly covering them.

Harvey asked the man standing out front, "What do you think of my duck?"

"That's one big duck!"

"What do you think of his neck?"

"I can't believe that skinny thing can hold up its head!"

With that, Timothy swallowed up the slob.

Harvey smiled to himself as he headed off up the street.

"This is going to be fun."

"Quack."

A HUNTING HE WILL GO
By Fleur Lind

"For Pete's sake, how much longer must I wait??" Harold muttered exasperatedly.

'This was not the plan at all. I was meandering about the house, doing my hunting and gathering things to share with the clan, and now I'm going to be late for lunch!'

Harold's thoughts ran away with him as he considered his options, but none came to mind.

'There is no way around or out of this mess. I'm stuck. I'm cornered.'

As question marks bumped into exclamation marks in a caricature fashion, and swam in a haphazard orbit around his head, he heard the continuing, gesticulating conversation taking place on speakerphone out on the back patio nearby.

'She's still jawing away, flapping those lips. The last time her sister called, she clocked up over an hour. At least she replaced the batteries in the wall clock in the kitchen. I can now keep track of the day.'

The conversation rambled along like tumbleweed.

"I know, Fran, I know. That's what I said, too. But it's not our call to make, she has to make her own mistakes, I guess."

"It could have been worse, it's not the end of the world, Martha, but it's not a great start either, is it?"

"That's very charitable of you. It's a darn good thing she didn't get caught!"

"Oh my God, yes! Imagine the ramifications if she had. She'd have been slammed with a hefty fine, and who would pay that?"

"Never mind the fine, the judge would throw the book at her."

"None of it bears thinking about. And what about us? What about the rest of the family? It's so embarrassing!"

"Well, let's hope she has learned a lesson, and it won't happen again."

"Yes, onward and upward."

'I have no idea what they are on about, nor do I care. What bothers me, there is no way out of this corner I am in. Why didn't she use fast-drying paint? How long will it take to dry? There's no way I'm walking across it; I'll get stuck - and that will be that.'

Harold thought he had time to get across to the breakfast bar before her paint roller got too close to him, but when Martha was on a mission, there was no holding her back

'Worse still, she's wearing that darn green bandana, so nothing is going to get in her way…except her sister with fresh gossip. So, she takes the call and settles on the lounger out on the patio. Meanwhile, the roller dries up, and I'm left waiting. So very inconsiderate!'

All that aside, Harold was still wondering how he was going to get down from his spot. It was going to become very tiresome in his current position beside the light shade covered with fly poo.

'That'll be the next thing - she'll take all the light coverings down and wash them or buy new flash ones. The new paint will show up the dust and whatever else.'

As Harold contemplated the complexities of this moment and life in general, there was a shift in gear out on the patio.

"Okay, Fran, I'll call you. I'm painting the ceiling, so I had better make a move. Let me know how you get on."

"Okay, Martha. You haven't got ideal weather for painting; this rain is meant to set in."

"Well, you know, when the mood hits me, it's hard to dampen the fire in my belly."

"True, take some antacids, that's good for heartburn, but nothing stops you when your mind is set."

"Yup. You know it! Talk soon! Bye."

Martha sighed as her mind churned over the details of her niece's misgivings. Having sat in the lounger so long, her body had a few creaks that weren't there before. Her warm muscles had cooled and set like the paint on her roller brush.

"Ouch! I should have sat in my massage chair instead. Now… where was I? I'll finish that patch, and that's the job done!"

She glanced at her phone as she entered the kitchen. "Darn it, there's only one bar left. I'd better charge it up before I ring her back."

Harold sighed. Any time today would be nice…

Martha examined the roller, with drying paint, which made it a little crusty to touch. "Darn it, but it's not worth starting with a new roller for that last little bit…"

As she looked up at that last bit, Harold held his breath.

Martha peered through a splotch of paint on the left lens of her glasses, making her almost cross-eyed. It impaired her vision somewhat; hence, she had not noticed Harold thus far.

"What's that?' She squinted, knowing it was futile to remove her glasses for a better examination of the large, dark round shape on the ceiling; her glasses aided her vision, so removal was inviting a complete blur.

"I hope it's not mold..." she muttered to herself, "what is it about renovations that creates more work than I started with?"

'Don't roll that wet, sticky, crusty roller over me, for goodness' sake!'

Harold said a prayer as his life flashed before his eyes. He also gave thanks to Pablo, who had shown him the benefits of praying when times get tough. The praying mantis community had become an ally to his clan.

As much as he tried to remain as still as possible, one of his legs was starting to cramp, so he painfully stretched it out.

"Ohhhhh…No! *Argh!* How long have you been there?"

'Martha, don't get me started! The answer is - too bloody long - so if you can hold the dramatics and assist me, I'll get out of your way, pronto!'

"Ohhh, creepy darn thing. I know you're not venomous, but you give me the heebie-jeebies. Oh, what to do?? You're so BIG! You're the size of a saucer! Oh, my God! Ray next door is away for the weekend, so he can't sort this out. Bugger!"

'Steady on, Martha, that's one for the swear jar!'

"Ohhh, I hate this…"

'Stop being such a sook! Go get the broom and I'll hop on…'

As if such a thing as telepathy existed between humankind and Arachna, Harold almost saw a lightbulb glow above Martha's messy bun. And this light bulb didn't have any fly poo on it.

"I know! I'll get the broom. Don't move! Wait right there!"

'Trust me, I'm not moving, but be quick about it, eh?'

Martha was on a new mission. The painting was no longer the prime focus. As she rushed to the cupboard in the laundry, kicking the basket filled with dry washing across the floor as she went, she pulled at the broom, which was at the back of the long, narrow cupboard behind the mop and bucket and other assorted cleaning equipment, all with long shafts or handles. Included in this disorganization was the vacuum cleaner with a bag of useful attachments. There was a crash as handles went this way and that, falling forward and landing on the floor like a game of Pick-Up Sticks.

"Bloody hell!"

'I heard that…are you going to be long?'

Martha appeared in the kitchen with a soft-bristled kitchen broom. The yard broom would be too heavy and awkward for the job at hand. Despite himself and his stressful dilemma, Harold chuckled. Martha looked quite a sight with her trusty bandana at a crooked angle to its normally composed status, and holding the broom as she did, all she needed was a black peaked hat.

"Right…" Martha had never felt so unsure.

'Well, that'll do the job nicely, just don't squash me…'

"Okay, pal, just… don't. fall. on. me," she stuttered as she gingerly raised the broom handle up to Harold.

Harold saw his moment. He was expecting the broom head to be his escape route, but okay, the handle was going to work equally well. Beggars couldn't be choosers. He took a big step, then a leap and landed on the end of the handle. He half slid - half ran down the length, heading straight for Martha's shaking hands.

All Martha could see was a massive Huntsman spider coming at speed, for her.

"ARRGGH!" Martha yelled, throwing the handle aside to avoid contact with Harold. The broom went one way, and Harold was flung to the other.

It was a bumpy landing as he hit the dinner table and skidded across the smooth, shiny surface.

Holy crap! No brakes! Harold wished the salt and pepper set were in his path to break his slide.

Finally, coming to a stop just before the tabletop edge, he righted himself and scrambled down the table leg to the sanctuary of the large, potted 'Elephant Ears' Begonia in the corner. Maybe the plant would lend one of its ears to his eventual vent when the shock had worn off. Wobbly knees were one thing, but when you had eight of them, it added to the stress levels. His heart was racing, and it was all he could do to stay focused and out of Martha's way.

"That went well, I wonder where he is now…"

Martha looked warily around the kitchen, hoping she would not encounter this creepy house guest again anytime soon.

Harold sighed and said another little prayer of thanks for his safe return to the ground.

'Be damned if I'm getting up on the ceiling again, and what a good job the cat wasn't playing any part in that drama. Her claws, teeth, and inquisitive playfulness would be the last straw!

Now to find out if they saved me any lunch!'

THE LOST PRINCESS
By Ellie Jay

The sun rose, bathing the empire in light. Sami stood, gazing out to the far reaches of the horizon, glowing golden.

As they should. As they would once again. She reached out and tugged, unleashing the flag to join the morning sun.

It was an act of defiance to start the new day with an old flag. But just as the flag was now forgotten and disregarded, the traditional greeting of the sun had been cast off by the degenerates and heathens who would only rise when their alarms forced them to.

That was, Sami knew, why this country, this once great empire, was crumbling. The apathy of these ungrateful fools.

She bowed low, greeting the sun as her ancestors would have, then stepped back to watch the flag – the imperial flag, not some mockery – flutter in the early morning breeze. And to consider her next move.

Last night, as she lay in bed, she had decided that this could not be allowed to continue. And her mind, clear of the distractions of her modern life, had presented her with the perfect solution.

She would restore the empire.

For while she still considered Ash-Kira the Gilded Empire, no one else did. They had cast aside that title and all it carried some 50 years earlier. It had been marred, her father claimed. A foolish claim, made by the weak. By those who had not understood that the emperor did what he did by the power invested in him by the Gods. They had no right to question it, let alone to exile the man and his family to the far-flung isle of Ki.

But they had. And now, in the empire's place, The Democratic Republic of Ash-Kira had… not risen. It would not to something as decisive or as powerful as rise. It had sat. Lazy, unambitious…

Sami did not plan to live that way.

But she had remembered, as she lay her head down, that she did not have to. The emperor himself had passed on. No doubt broken-hearted by the betrayal his own people had inflicted upon him.

But there was another. The heir to the Gilded Empire lived. Princess Marisha was waiting on the lonely isle of Ki, for a devoted subject to restore her to the throne.

Sami had vowed to do just that.

Soon. Very soon. But first, alas, there was work to be done. She sighed and turned away, away from the sun, the stretching land before her, and the flag. Back to her apartment.

It was a modest one, like many others in the capital block. Once, a grand building would have stood here. One built by people who loved their Gods and their Empire. Who worked long and hard to honor them.

Now, a soulless street of apartment blocks stood, built for businessmen who wanted the job done as cheaply and as quickly as possible.

Sami shook her head. It was disgusting. What had life come to?

There was worse, she knew, yet to come. She had to prepare for the day in this country, this disgraceful place.

And how did one do that? With breakfast. One that was not worked for and earned in the betterment of the Empire but automated by democratic technology. Her food, kept cold by their whims and heated by them too.

She chewed the Gods-forsaken meal down. If there had been an alternative, then she would have gladly taken it, but she was without choice in this horrible place. She even forced herself to down the gritty, foul liquid that the machines in every apartment, every office block, every building across the land made.

She would have benefitted from the natural, old ways instead. Pure milk from the beasts raised on the fresh, green grass of the Gilded Empire. Water fresh from the springs blessed by the emperor's own hand.

But there was no choice. The foul muck brought energy, unnatural, ungodly energy that was nevertheless needed to survive the awful democratic notion she must submit to next.

The 9-5.

She had to go to work. At an office job. For a company.

How did this glorify her Gods? Her Empire? She should be finding, restoring and serving the lost Princess. Not filing paperwork and sending emails.

Such horrors that life had come to.

But today, she had a new resolve with which to endure. She would book time off and use it to fly to Ki. To find the Princess.

Then this horror would be over. These high-rise monstrosities in which the citizens of the Empire were forced to live would be demolished and replaced with real houses. There would be no rent, because their new Empress would own the land and the homes. She would house them, provide for them and they would work for her, not a cold, soulless corporation.

Yes, everything had been better when life had been arranged for them by a begin ruler. Now there were too many fools involved. Bumbling idiots in suits elected by people even stupider than they were.

The good old days were needed, before their great country fell further into ruin. And she would be the one to bring them back, Sami assured herself as she forced the final bite of her breakfast past her lips.

She wiped the smears from her face, grabbed her briefcase from behind the door and hurried out, into the bustling city. The only things racing faster than the traffic were her mind and her heart, filled with what she was about to do.

Brriiing! Brriiiiing!

The alarm clock's shrill ring shattered the morning peace. Taron groaned and rolled over, thumping the thing so hard that it clattered to the floor.

Brrriinnng!

He swore and was rewarded with a soft chuckle.

"Really, Dear? Every morning? If you would let me take that side, I'd be able to cope with it without resorting to that kind of language."

His wife was sitting up beside him, an expression of bemused good humor on her face.

"You love my language," he muttered, rubbing his eyes. "Anyway, if you sleep on this side, you sleep-walk. We only put the damn bed against the wall after… the incident, remember?"

"Oh, hush. That was twenty years ago. Walking's hard enough when I'm awake now," she chided him softly.

He pulled himself upright too and looked over at her. Her golden-brown eyes were bright with laughter, but he knew it was only half a joke. Her face was worn, lined with wrinkles, and he had noticed her ever-present limp growing more pronounced.

His own hips were complaining at the way he was sat. He sighed. A further lay-in was out of the question, even if that damn clock hadn't disturbed his peace.

He leaned down, wincing as he did, and seized the thing. Switching it off, he placed it back on the bedside table, then turned and kissed Shia's soft cheek.

"I know, my sweet. But come, let's force ourselves up and enjoy another day. Wasn't that the idea behind the stupid clock in the first place?"

Shia grinned. "That was for you. I've always been an early riser, but here I am, trapped by your bulk," she poked his stomach, "besides, I want us to be able to things together. To enjoy the time that we have left."

Her face clouded over with thoughtfulness, and he frowned.

"Don't talk like that. We've got plenty of time. And we've been so lucky with what we've had."

She nodded, cheering slightly. "We have, haven't we? Come on, let's have breakfast and then walk down to see the sea. It's beautiful this time of year."

The couple rose, albeit slowly, to begin their day. On the way to kitchen, Shia stopped and picked up an old, framed photograph. She caught her husband's eye.

"Don't you wonder...?"

"Where they are now? Every day. But they made their choice. And we ours. If ever they need us, they'll know where to find us."

"And if we need them? Or if I wanted to say goodbye, before..."

He put his arm around her waist, stroking her hip and tutting. "You really mustn't think that way, my flower. We'll go on like this forever."

"Gods willing." She set the photograph down and continued their walk to the kitchen.

Sami's journey to work was uneventful, if frustrating. It bugged her to see the vapid morons bumbling through life. It bothered her to walk past bland buildings, without imperial flags fluttering and shrines to the Gods.

No one believed any more. Even her own family thought she was stark-raving mad for caring about the traditions of the country. And they were older, supposedly wiser. After all, they should remember the old ways.

She herself was barely thirty years old. But her parents, in their sixties now, should know better. Certainly, her grandparents ought to. It disgusted her to see the pity in their eyes. To hear them mutter that she didn't know what she was talking about.

Anyone would think their lives under the old Emperor had been bad. Ungrateful, all of them.

She pushed through the doors of the office complex, a blast of air conditioning smacking her in the face.

That was another modern mockery. Why could they not sweat as the Gods had intended? Because people were too weak, that was why.

Still, the place wasn't all bad. It was here that she had discovered the truth. Become enlightened.

When she had arrived here, she had only been a young intern, fitting the role in alongside her university studies in the hopes of gaining experience. Which, tragically, she had needed. She knew nothing about life.

For one thing, she had never given politics a second thought. But now, suddenly thrust from the sheltering, middle-class home of her parents, into the real world, she was free to discover life.

And to be discovered. Ms. Arino, the head of her department, had seen something in her. Seeing that she was ready to learn the truth.

Now, she was on the cusp of fulfilling her mentor's dreams. All she needed to do was get the other woman to approve her time off.

And she knew she would. How could she not? How could Arino not want to find the lost Princess just as much as she did?

Spurred on by these thoughts, she dropped her briefcase onto her chair and strode towards the older woman's office.

As Sami pushed open the door, she was met by a welcoming smile.

"Good morning. Come in. What can I do for you?" Ms. Arino closed the file on her desk and sat back in her chair.

Giving Sami her full attention. The younger woman beamed. "I need some time off."

Her boss looked at her curiously. "You seem pretty excited about this. Last minute holiday or…" she glanced at her stomach, "some news you want to share?"

Sami flushed. "No. No. Nothing like that. But I'm… I'm going to the Isle of Ki."

The older woman's smile froze. "Why? There's nothing there."

"There's something." Sami checked over her shoulder, making sure she had closed the door behind her. And no one was watching them.

"I'm finally doing it. Completing our mission. I need to find the lost Princess."

Ms. Arino's file slid to the floor as the older woman got to her feet.

Taron sat on the golden sand and watched as his wife took slow, careful steps down to the shore.

She had struggled with their walk today. By the time breakfast had been over and done with, her enthusiasm had already waned.

There was much on her mind, that was plain to see. But they had made this far, arm-in-arm. And she seemed cheered, once they had reached the beach.

She had insisted on walking all the way to the shoreline. But here, the sand sloped and shifted, and his hips ached as he tried to pick his way across it. So, he sat down.

And she had continued on, striking out on her own.

Now, she reached the water's edge and stood, looking out across the crystal-clear sea, to the buildings rising on the distant horizon.

And spoke; a soft, whispered word that, had it not been whipped up the beach by the fresh coastal wind, he would never have heard.

It was almost dark when Sami left the office that evening. The sun was setting in the distance. But she was so wrapped up in her thoughts that she barely noticed.

She had been distracted all day; knew she had done a poor job. But how could she not? How was she supposed to continue after such sudden, blind-siding betrayal?

Ms. Arino had refused her leave. Not only that, but she had seemed positively furious to be asked. Her face had contorted as she stood up and she had leaned across the desk, getting too close to Sami.

"That woman, that witch, is no Princess. She would destroy the Empire's legacy out of her own selfishness. Go to see her, and you destroy our cause forever."

Her friendly, welcoming boss and mentor had vanished. In her place, this dark spirit with her dire warnings of destruction.

But how? How could such a thing be true? And how could Ms. Arino know?

Unless she had visited the lost Princess herself? But any attempts to continue that conversation were lost, Sami had known, just from looking into her eyes.

The message was clear. The isle of Ki held nothing.

… Except the answers to a thousand questions. For Sami was even more confused now than she had been when Ms. Arino had first raised the subject of the Empire.

A plan, formed from the broken remnants of that which she had thought true, formed in her mind.

She would take sick leave and catch the first flight to Ki. After all, her Princess was disgraced and her mentor a whole new person. There must at least be some answers on that island.

Two days later, her flight took off. It was early morning, light just beginning to pour into the world.

She hadn't been back to work since her conversation with Ms. Arino. She'd claimed a sickness bug. But in reality, she had spent the last 48 hours gathering as much information as possible about Ki, and the lost Princess it harbored.

There was precious little to know, but the Isle was small and wouldn't take long to search. And she did know that Marisha, the Princess, would be seventy-three now. She was reputed to still live on the isle, in an old royal residence. The only one the emperor's family had been allowed to keep.

It shouldn't be hard to spot a grand palace on a tiny island.

Sami smiled to herself as the plane rose into the sky. Finally, she would have the answers to all her questions, problems and woes.

Ki was even smaller than she had imagined. The 'airport' where her flight landed looked like someone's garden shed. She wrinkled her nose.

What a disgraceful place. How could anyone have cast their glorious royal family into this place?

At least, Sami thought it would be simple to find a royal residence in this hole in the ground. She stepped out of the so-called airport and scanned the horizon.

To her dismay, there was no golden palace rising up over the beach. Just a row of cheerful little houses, painted up like beach huts.

And sand. Miles and miles of golden sand.

She swore as she stood, looking hopelessly across the landscape.

Nearby, an elderly man chuckled. She turned to stare him down, but instead she was struck by the tears pouring down his face.

He was laughing at her, but he was wracked by grief at the same time.

"Are you okay?" The words left her mouth almost unbidden, instinct taking over from the contempt she was used to showing people.

"My wife passed away yesterday. She always used to scold me for my language. Then we'd laugh…"

"I'm… sorry?" The words were unnatural, but she found she meant them, as she set her case down on the sands and stepped towards the old man.

"Don't be, girlie, don't be. She's free now. *Lee'ma*. That's what she said to me, in the last few hours."

Her eyes widened. The word was from the old faith. I found peace, it meant. But no one would use it now. No one but this man's wife. An old woman, living out her days on this island…

He took a handkerchief from his pocket and wiped his eyes, then smiled, watching her incredulous face.

"Yes. She was a princess to the last, my Shia. Ironic, considering she never wanted the crown. Not after what her father put the family through."

She frowned. "Marisha didn't want to be a princess? But…"

He shook his head. "I've heard all the arguments. When our children found out, they were furious. Said she robbed them of their heritage. They took all the money she had left from her father's legacy and went to the mainland. Shia hoped… She thought they might call when she was dying. But they only wanted glory. And she only wanted to live a normal life. At last."

Sami stared out, across the water.

"You don't understand it, do you?"

"I'm beginning to. *Lee'ma…*" she turned, meeting his gaze again. "I know you. You were the Grand Vizor. Lord Taho…"

"Was. Once. Not now," he smiled.

Sami felt herself smile, too. For the first time in years, it felt real. But there was one puzzle piece left.

"Ms. Arino said the world was stupid to forget the Empire. Then she said I shouldn't come here… That Marisha was a selfish woman."

The old man shook his head. "Ah, my would-be princess. My daughter… She got into your head too, I see. Take my advice, child. Move on. We managed to."

As one, they looked out across the golden beach. At peace, at last.

NO CENSORSHIP PLEASE, WE'RE BRITISH

By Alec Sillifant

Tina tugged at the edges of her white lace Basque, checking everything was stowed away just enough to cause the desired effect. She doubted her groom, Derek, waiting in the bedroom of the Honeymoon Suite, would be making such detailed preparations on her behalf.

Her wedding had gone perfectly to plan and now it was all going to culminate in a night of passion she would remember, and cherish, for the rest of her life. With one last tousle of her hair, she turned and, not knowing why, rapped gently at the bathroom door.

"Are you ready, darling?"

"Hell, yeah," came the reply.

Sheepishly, Tina opened the door and exposed herself to her mate. She had been right; the only preparations Derek had bothered with were a glass of champagne in each hand and an erection.

"Well?"

Derek leered. "Wow…that is hot," he said.

Tina sashayed across the room until she was face to face with Derek.

"Hello, husband," she said, pressing her belly against his obvious excitement. "I think it's time we got the real celebrations started."

Slowly she got to her knees and, gazing into Derek's, eyes leant forward to--

The door to the Honeymoon Suite opened to reveal a man in a suit, he held a golden badge in one hand and a clipboard in the other. The badge was raised for inspection, a beacon of his authority to be present.

"Hold it right there. Inspector Steam, Interpol."

Derek's mouth dropped open. Tina's mouth dropped open even wider than it had been. The newlyweds looked at each other with shock in their eyes, both wondering what the other had done to attract the attention of such a powerful law enforcing agency.

Inspector Steam pocketed his badge, closed the door and strode across the room, hand stretched out in greeting.

"Hi, you must be…" he consulted the clipboard, "…Tina and Derek Goodson."

Derek automatically took the hand offered and shook it.

"Yes…but Interpol? What does Interpol want with us?"

Tina got to her feet and did her best to hide her modesty. "Derek, what have you done?"

"I haven't done anything."

Steam laughed. "No, no, you've got it all wrong. This happens all the time. I'm not with *that* Interpol; I'm with *the* Interpol. The Intercourse Police."

"The who?" said Derek. He reached for the bath robe on the bed, to hide his obvious love for Tina.

"Oh, don't worry about that, sir," said Steam, a wide grin on his face, "I've seen plenty of them in my job. And you might like to know, you're in the top ten percentile."

"Thank you?" said Derek.

"You could say, they're the hardest part of my job." Steam chuckled… alone.

"Can you please tell me what you think you're doing here?" said Tina, her mental composure returning despite her state of undress.

Steam shook his head. "Don't tell me, another couple who wasn't given the leaflet."

"Leaflet? What leaflet?" said Derek.

"The 'Authorized Acts of the Wedding Night' leaflet," said Steam.

Tina frowned. "I don't understand?"

"Last week," began Steam, obviously happy to enlighten, "the government brought in the 'Authorized Acts of the Wedding Night Act' to ensure that any activities between two consenting, and married, adults stay within a licensed and legal format. So, I-"

"That's ridiculous," said Tina.

"Ridiculous, maybe. The law, undoubtedly," said the Inspector. "I am here to ensure you comply with the letter, and spirit, of the law. Do you understand?"

Derek and Tina both gave muted nods.

"Good," said Steam. He raised his clipboard and slapped his free hand on it. "First you will need a 'Coitus License'."

"What the hell is a 'Coitus License'?" said Derek, his love rapidly subsiding beneath the bath robe.

Steam raised an eyebrow. "Fairly obvious I would have thought, the clue's in the title."

"I think we all understand that" said Tina, "what I think Derek is saying is, why would we *need* it?"

"It's the law," said Steam.

"So, we need a license to have sex?" said Derek.

"Bingo," said Steam, smiling.

"But we've had sex before," said Tina, her voice defiant.

"That may be," said Steam, "but now you're married you need a license." He could tell by the look of incredulity on the faces of the happy couple that he would have to expand. "It's like riding a bike-"

"I beg your pardon?!" said Tina.

"No, no, Mrs. Goodson, a bicycle…I wasn't inferring that you…anyway," said Steam, a little flustered, "you can ride round on your bicycle all you want with few regulations whilst an amateur but as soon as you join a cycling club, and want to try it out professionally, you need a license."

"We need a license for sex because we're married?" said Derek.

"Yes," said the Inspector, beaming with pride that he'd got his point across.

Tina looked at her husband. "What should we do?"

"I don't think we have a choice," said Derek, shrugging his shoulders.

Tina bit her bottom lip and sucked air in audibly. "Okay, you'd best issue us with a Coitus License, then."

"Grand," said Steam, ripping off the front page from his clipboard. "That will be ten pounds please."

"What?!" said Derek.

"Oh, just pay the Jobsworth," said Tina, as she rubbed her hand through her hair. "Get him out of our honeymoon as quickly as possible."

Derek strode over to his morning suit, which was rented and so hung neatly on a hanger in the wardrobe, and retrieved his wallet.

"There you go, ten pounds."

"Thank you, Mr. Goodson, there's your Basic Coitus License."

"Basic?" said Derek. He studied the license. "Why basic, we can legally have sex now can't we?"

"Indeed, you can, Mr. Goodson…in the missionary position."

"Just the missionary position?" said Tina.

"Yes. It is only the Basic Coitus License, Mrs. Goodson," said Steam.

"Which suggest there are other…err…more *advanced*, licenses to be had?" said Derek.

"That is correct."

"That allow more than just the missionary position?" said Tina.

"That is also correct."

There was a momentary pause as Tina and Derek waited for Steam to expand on his statement.

"Well?" said Tina.

"Oh, you're interested in a more…diverse package," said Steam, as realization hit.

"Yes," said Derek, "why wouldn't we?"

"Well, it just seemed like…you know…you don't look the type…" said Steam, before waving his hand dismissively.

"Of course, of course, who am I to judge? Righty-oh then. We have the 'Bow-Wow License' then the 'Licky-Licky License' and finally the 'Fifty Shades of License'. That last one really is no holes barred, if you get my drift."

"I think we do, thank you, Inspector," said Tina. "I assume these licenses go up in price?"

"No, some of them go down," said Steam, adding a second of laughter. "No, that's just a little departmental joke, they do go up in price the higher up the range you go."

"How much is the 'Fifty Shade of License?" said Tina.

"Whoa, you're a lucky boy, Mr. Goodson," said Steam, with a wink for Derek. "It's two hundred pounds, Mrs. Goodson."

"Two hundred quid!" said Derek.

Tina placed a hand on her lace enhanced hip and stared deep into the eyes of her newly acquired husband.

"Oh, and I suppose you have got something better to spend *that* kind of money on?!"

Derek swallowed. "No darling, of course not, cheap at half the price."

He dug into his wallet and counted off nine twenties and a ten.

"Thank you very much," said Steam and he handed Derek a guilt edged certificate made of wafer-thin leather.

"It's a great investment, I'm sure you'll get years of pleasure from it. Though I should warn you it is non-transferable should your relationship break down."

"Nice to know," said Tina. Her forced smile said otherwise.

"And there is a replacement fee should you lose it or get stains on it or something."

Tina and Derek stared at the inspector in silence.

"Anyway," said Steam, "I'll get out of your hair now. I'm sure you've got other things you'd like to be getting on with. *Pressing* matters, as it were."

"Goodbye, Inspector Steam," said Tina. She indicated the Honeymoon Suite's door with her open hand.

"I'll see myself out," said Steam, as he backed away from the couple all smiles. "Congratulations and may you have a long and happy life together."

Steam closed the door behind him.

"Well, that was strange," said Derek.

"Strange; how come you didn't know about that?"

"Me? You looked just as clueless as me."

"Yes…maybe it had something to do with me organizing the cars and flowers and bridesmaids and the catering and my dress and your suit and making sure your mother was happy and booking the church and the honeymoon. Maybe it slipped my mind to find out about a license, I had never heard of until ten minutes ago, while I was worrying if you might hurt yourself as you sat on your fucking arse doing nothing!"

Derek thought his ears might be bleeding. He was certain his mouth was hanging open and that his eyes would shame any rabbit caught in headlights.

"Sorry?"

"Sorry!?" screamed Tina. "You're sorry?!"

Derek tried a lopsided grin and shrug, going for the 'stupid bloke' plea.

Tina closed her eyes and breathed in and out deeply through her nose for a few moments. She gathered her thoughts.

'This is my wedding night; I have dreamed of this for years. I am not going to have ruined by a stupid man…two stupid men.' She rolled head to relieve the tension knotting her neck and opened her eyes. "I'm sorry too," she said, "I'm still a little bit tense from the excitement of the day and I think that license thing pushed me over the edge."

Derek stepped forward and put his arms around her. "It's okay my love, I understand."

Tina fought hard to ignore the bait of pure patronization.

"I tell you what," said Derek, breaking free of the clinch, "the name's Goodson, Derek Goodson and I've got a license to thrill."

He waved the leather document.

"Why, Mr. Goodson, is that a pistol under your bathrobe or are you just pleased to see me?"

"Careful, Mrs. Goodson, it's loaded. It could blow your head off."

"Oh, I don't know," said Tina, returning to her knees, "I think you may find *I* can blow *your* head off."

She clamped one hand around Derek's stiff member and leant in--

The Honeymoon Suite's door burst open again.

"Stop right there! You could have someone's eye out with that thing. It needs a hi-vis jacket on it at least, probably a guard rail too. I'll have to do a full assessment. And you, young lady, should be wearing safety goggles."

"What the fuck, this time?" said Derek, as he reached for the bathrobe again.

The intruder, who wore a yellow hard hat to top off his ensemble of paint-splattered boiler suit and steel toecap rigger boots, flipped open a wallet to reveal an identity card.

"Mr. Bridges; Health and Safety Executive. Have you got a license to operate that lifting equipment?"

Tina screamed and ran back into the sanity of the bathroom.

DOG TRAINING METHODS
By Neil Noble

One morning, I was sitting and eating my breakfast, half reading the paper and half speculating about a short story I'm writing on how dogs train their humans. In the middle of my reverie, my schnauzer, Bandit, nosed my knee under the table. When I looked down, he was staring at me intently.

"What do you want?" I asked, pretending – hoping - that he understood me.

His response was the same quiet, intense stare as always while standing as rigid as a statue.

"When are you going to learn to speak so you can tell me what you want?"

When he didn't respond, I patted my leg with a resigned sigh.

"Up?"

That's when he wagged his tail. When I put him onto my lap, Bandit immediately turned his back to me, sat down, and stared out of the large window in front of the kitchen table. People often walked up and down our dead-end street. Every time it would set off the frenzied barking alarm warning us of potential trespassers and other evildoers.

As Bandit sat on my lap watching people come and go, it didn't occur to me that he was doing his own daydreaming. I suspect he was remembering his own birth family, now scattered who knows where.

"Thank you, Mom, for teaching me how to train my two-legged animals," Bandit probably thought.

Happy Birthday, pups! Look at you. All of two months old, eating solid food, full of yourselves and ready for whatever the world throws at you.

Okay, children listen up. Bandit, stop biting Annabelle. Sit still like Charlee and David. This is serious.

Within the next few weeks, two-legged animals will come here to take you away from me. No Bandit, mommy is not happy about it either. You will be scared and lonely for a while, but I hope all of you will have kind and gentle two-legged animals to take care of you. You will get used to your new space. You might have it all to yourself or another of our kind will already be there. Remember, most of the time, these two-legged animals love to have us around, and they will give us scratches and belly rubs without our having to ask.

If you're the only one, you'll have to train your new two-legged animals, like I've trained the ones in this big crate. They're not as smart as some I've seen, but they are easy to work with. I've taught them a few tricks, like when to let me outside for bathroom breaks and when to feed me. They will take me for a ride in the car when I ask. They will fetch my toys or treats no matter where I leave them. They play with me, give me tummy rubs and scratches, and they go to sleep when I tell them it's time.

Darwin, stop wagging your butt at me and turn around! Now pay attention, all of you!

The first thing I need to teach you is how to make them understand you. They don't understand our language, and they don't like it when we talk too much or too loudly. Instead, you'll have to stand and stare at them for however long it takes to get their attention. Make sure you stand in front of them; that means wherever their nose is pointing. If they turn their head, then you move also. Eventually, they will speak their language to you. They will begin to list the things they know we like: go outside? walk? treat? car ride?

When they say the right word, wag your tail faster and perk up your ears. Then, reward them by licking their hand or face. The more you lick, the faster they will learn. You'll also need to teach them about bathroom breaks as soon as possible. They should let you outside of their big crate about every 30 degrees of the yellow ball's movement (about two hours).

Yes, I know it's a long time but do your best to hold it even if you're playing and excited. If you do have an accident inside their crate, look as sad as possible. They'll understand you're sorry. If you need to go outside sooner, stare at them as I explained or go sit in front of the door and speak loudly a few times to get their attention. When they finally understand, wag your tail. That's also their reward for obeying you. It's okay to lick them as well.

So, do you think we should talk about food next? Oh, so *now* I have your undivided attention? Okay, okay. Stop yapping at me. My two-legged animals feed me two times a day. Once, soon after the yellow ball is high enough to see, and again when it drops down and can't be seen anymore. You'll have to teach yours to follow the same pattern.

After a good night's sleep, jump up onto the soft place where they sleep, if you can. You're still small so you may have to speak loudly to get their attention. Scramble up and lick their faces. Then quickly go to the other end of their sleep place. If they do not obey immediately, do it again. Bounce up and down once or twice and spin in circles until they get up and let you go outside. When they bring you back into their big crate, go and stand by your food spot. Maybe use a quiet voice so they understand the food is gone and you want more.

Wait a minute. Where did Darwin go? DARWIN! You had better get your tail back in here! Don't make me come after you! Charlee, did you just knock over Bandit?

Now, for me, one of the best parts of living with a two-legged animal is riding in the car. That's the big thing that sits outside. You get inside of the car, and it moves while you stand still. No, Charlee, I don't know how it does that.

When I'm in the car, I get to look at the outside from a different point of view. I'm higher up and I get to go to and see other places. When the car stops moving, we all get out and walk around. There are so many new sights, sounds, and scents. Sometimes, we go to a big, open area with a fence around it, where many of our kind gather. Sometimes we talk about the big crate where we live. But usually it's about the two-legged animals we live with and how to train them; what works best. Other times, there's a place with very soft, light colored earth beside water that goes out farther than we can see. I highly recommend the car. If any of you want to try it out, here's what you do. Start by standing in front of the door. Speak two or three times. If that doesn't get the attention of the two-legged animals, go sit in front of them and speak. Now move towards the door but stay in their line of sight. Sit and speak again. If they don't understand, go back, sit in front of them again, and speak. They will get it eventually. But the tricky part is they won't know if you want to go to the bathroom, go for a walk, or ride in the car.

When you get outside, walk towards the car. If they pull you away or call your name, just sit down. We must train them to know the difference between 'bathroom', 'leash', and 'ride'. It's hard work, but worth it, my little ones. They will understand, eventually, because of your training of them.

You'll use the same method to teach the two-legged animals to fetch lost toys or treats. Stand in front of them and speak softly a few times. When you have their attention, walk in the direction you want them to go. Then turn and speak again, then walk away again. Keep doing this until you're where you need to be. If your treat or toy is under something, pretend to dig for it. If you just want to play with your two-legged animal, stand over your toy, or lie down so only your head covers the toy, then speak. Repeat this as often as necessary until they learn.

Another trick is how to teach your two-legged animals when to go to sleep. At first, they will ignore the white ball when it is high in the night sky. They'll be busy with other things, and they'll be ignoring you. Of course, this is wrong, Annabelle! They need to understand this and adjust their attitude and behavior to always be ready to do what you want to do. How you train them is very important. They are capable of learning. It may take a little bit of time. Just don't give up. Remember, they are learning a new language, and some two-legged animals are smarter than others. Be patient. When it's time to go to bed, sit in front of them and stare. When they finally look at you, lie down. If they ignore you, sit up and speak. When they look at you again, lie down again. Keep doing this until they recognize "bed".

All right, that's enough for now. Over the next few sun cycles, watch what I do. You need to learn these training methods before you leave me, little ones.

Oh dear, I think I've exhausted my babies. They are about to fall asleep where they sit. I'll just nudge them all together. There, now I can lie down with my paws around them to protect them.

Bandit had been sitting on my lap, interrupting my breakfast for more than fifteen minutes, when he started to yawn. Without moving his body, he twisted his head to look at me. Then he stood up, turned a bit, and jumped down to the floor. Seeming to ignore me, he walked over to his food bowl, sniffed at it, took a sip of water instead, then just walked out of the kitchen.

As Bandit walked away, he thought 'these are pretty good two-legged animals. They need a bit more training but they're keepers. Thanks again, Mom.'

THE POETRY OF LOVE
By Mason Bushell

"She looked into his eyes, and he finally realized

Her words were never lies

Truth tumbling with every tear

Shaking with cold fear"

The night was warm and sultry beside the lake. Lord Donthorne was hosting his annual summer masquerade ball beneath moody grey skies this year.

Malcolm, dressed in his finest black suit, was playing the role of waiter. There was no other way he'd gain entry into such a lavish event. He'd been serving flutes of expensive Don Pérignon champagne in the gardens when he heard her. The poet's soft, sweet and yet melancholy voice sent chills down his spine.

"She really loved him

He was going so far away

She was lonely without him

His kiss said it'd be okay."

Wending his way between the regal guests, he searched for her. He passed between ladies dripping in gold and diamonds. Gentlemen flashing Rolex watches as they mooched about wearing extravagant Italian suits. Each guest hid his or her identity behind sexy or scary masks of jewels and feathers. Beneath arbors draped in grapevines and passion flowers. Around the marble fountain toward the fringes of the garden, he searched.

"He'd be back for her

He'd be back for sure."

Malcolm came upon the folly. A striking stone structure made to look like a grand tower, although nothing more than a hollow façade. This evening, the entrance was adorned with gold drapes. Between them, holding a lantern, he found her.

The flickering light glinted upon her long platinum-blonde hair. She appeared dark and sultry, dressed in a black cape which flared like elegant wings as she curtseyed to gentle applause.

Malcolm felt his chest heave with desire. She was beautiful in her tiny black dress and fishnet stockings, revealing bare feet. 'Must you hide behind your black sparkly mask? Can it really be you?' He thought.

"May we have some champagne?" asked a gentleman with a fine moustache.

"Certainly, Sir." Malcolm flourished his silver tray. With his last glass served, he bowed away and glanced back towards the folly. The poet was gone.

Malcolm spun a frustrated circle; he had to find her again. If she were Harmony, he had a chance to repair the fractured rhythms of his broken heart.

"Malcolm. You have no right to be standing here and still with an empty tray. There are more canapés and wine to be served," demanded Mr. Richter, the Donthorne family Butler and manager of the event.

"I'm sorry. I have to do something," Malcolm thrust his tray at the butler. "I'll get back to work soon," he added before walking away.

The butler stood there open-mouthed, unable to form a word of resistance.

The poet had gone down toward the lake.

Had it not been for her lantern, Malcolm might never have seen her again. His heart pounded in his chest, keeping rhythm with the tension building in his lungs as his eyes fell upon her back. He ran down the lawn to catch up with her. Then, realizing a fast approach might scare her, he forced himself to walk with decorum.

The lady padded onto the fishing dock. She perched at the end with her feet hanging over the edge of the wooden deck. Even in the way she held her lantern before her, it was clear her soul was aching.

Malcolm came to a stop at the edge of the dock. He felt his soul reaching out to caress hers. It was his fault she was gazing over the waters of the natural lake so pensive, so mournful. Maybe a poem he wrote with her would help.

"Something about the way she dances

Makes my skin tingle as my heart prances

Sweetheart, that's how I feel.

When you're near, my pains heal"

The lady turned to face him. At once, her pretty face creased with recognition and sadness beneath her mask.

"Malky?"

'I'm truly Mesmerized by her

My soul simply approves

She owns my love, of that I'm sure

It's something in the way she moves,"

Malcolm finished the second stanza and nodded.

"Why are you here?" she asked, her voice shaking with tears.

"Hello, Harmony. I thought I was here to work as a waiter. I was wrong. Fate brought me here — brought me back to you. All those years ago, when I left home. When my parents forced me to move away to Kent, I never wanted to go. I left my heart and soul with you."

"Oh, Malky. I can't believe you're here."

Malcolm had remained a respectful distance. "May I sit with you?"

"Please," she patted the dock beside her.

"Thank you. I thought you'd run the second you saw me." Malcolm stopped behind her. "You're easily the most beautiful lady here tonight. You glow brighter than any of them."

Harmony reached for his hand and drew him down beside her.

"Thanks, Malky. I cried for weeks when you left. I didn't know if I'd ever see you again. Life has been so hard without —"

"I'm here now. Believe me, I'm so sorry for leaving you." Malcolm eased her mask from her face and gazed into her emerald eyes as he held her. "You feel that?"

"What?" Harmony blinked just once, transfixed by him.

Malcolm took a deep breath, infusing his senses with Jasmine, vanilla and rose notes of her perfume.

"Healing. Being close to you, holding you, is healing my soul. If I promise never to leave again, Harmony, will you let me stay?"

Harmony gave a beautiful smile as she lay her head on his shoulder, permitting him to cuddle her close.

"I'm never letting you go again," she said.

Shifting his gaze to the shimmering lake, Malcolm felt years of pain melting away. "Then I'll be whole—"

"Malcolm! I told you to get back to work. Now, I find you romancing with the guests. You're—"

"I quit." Malcolm cut him off.

Harmony looked stunned in his arms.

"You disrespectful young—"

"I'm sorry, Mr. Richter. Sometimes there are things in life which are far more important than work. Things, far more important than serving stupidly expensive champagne to overpaid, over-endowed snobs."

Malcolm stood with Harmony and held her from behind

"But—but you were being paid well. I don't understand," Richter stuttered, looking shocked.

"I could be making as much money as these rich people, and I still wouldn't be happy. Harmony and I went to school together a few years ago. When I was forced to move away, I lost her. I split my heart and broke hers when I left. In giving me this job, you brought me back to her. You see, I would choose Harmony and happiness over money any day. If losing this job is finding happiness with the only lady I could ever love, then I quit."

Harmony reached over her shoulder and kissed him. "Thank you, Malky. I think it's time we left."

"Lead the way, my lady." Malcolm took her hand and left the dock, walking right past his former boss.

"Wait!" Mr. Richter removed and polished his glasses. "What you say is true. I lost the love of my life by following my dream of working. As a result, I never became a restaurateur and ended up a loveless butler instead. The job is still yours if you want it. Go home now, look after Harmony, and I hope to see you both here next weekend." Richter replaced his glasses and strode away.

Harmony giggled as she faced Malcolm. "I think we pulled his heartstrings."

"I'm not surprised. You've been playing sweet music on mine since I heard you reciting your poem." Malcolm smoothed her hair as their lips met.

Behind them, the lake was lit up by a thousand glittering sparks as a fireworks display began. The couple barely noticed as their souls united in love once more.

DYING WISH

By Betty Mermelstein

It could have been cooler in the waiting room. Carol called it the waiting room only because it was a precursor to the next step, the final step.

A tiny table, barely big enough to set on it the meals that had probably aided in her demise, was at her left, swung halfway into position over the bed so that through her left eye she saw only its underside. The table now held her sister Tina's gigantic purse, a bit of which she could also see. She often wondered what would happen to Tina if she were ever minus the purse. Would her arm drag past her waist in search of the missing weight, and would she start convulsing for lack of tissues, pills, and lipstick? And there was Tina herself, her body cascading in folds around her like a huge rubber chew toy that any Labrador retriever would love to get hold of. She sat on the other side of the bed away from the table that held her purse. Kind of like bookends, but without the support.

Tina was talking to Jeremy. It was more like yelling. Tina yelling. Jeremy yelling back. Jeremy guffawing. Tina slapping her own leg, setting off a rippling effect, playing up and down her body.

Jeremy was sitting in the corner, but the cramped room made it so that he was also right at the end of the bed. Jeremy was first in the birth line, which tended to make him more of an aloof near-adult figure. The fifteen-year age difference hadn't helped. Tina's introduction to the world had followed five years after Jeremy's.

The table also held a plastic cup of water offering its cure for dehydration through the means of a bendable straw, which Carol could have bent toward her mouth if only she had had the power to do so. She pictured herself performing the task but couldn't actually do it. The scenario of forming the word 'water' wasn't any more real than reaching for the cup. She heard herself say it inside her head, but what air puffed away from her lips was inaudible.

"Oh, look," Tina pointed toward her sister in wonder. "I think she's trying to say something."

Tina's face loomed over Carol's.

"I'll bet you're not comfortable, are you?" she asked and judged all at once. "Jeremy, help me move her. She's trying to get over on one side and she doesn't have the strength to do it."

I am? Carol asked herself incredulously. No, Tina, THAT is not what I need.

She felt Tina's ham-like mitts under her hips while Jeremy maneuvered himself around to spatula-lift her shoulders.

"Look at this," Tina muttered in a conspiratorial tone.

I can hear you, Carol thought. For some reason, my hearing is still just fine.

"She's like a stick off the branch of a tree! I could have moved her myself."

You've really got to stop second guessing what I want, Carol silently warned Tina.

She was rotated to her side so that her lips couldn't have been any further from that drink.

No, Tina…and Jeremy…you follower!

She ended up staring at the Venetian blinds on the window: the Venetian blinds she knew would not be opened to her so that she could catch a last glimpse of the earth.

"There we go," Tina said more loudly. "Just what you need. Put a pillow behind her, Jeremy, so she won't roll back over."

You really ought to stop trying to direct my life - what's left of it. Always telling me what not to wear, how my short hair looks good on other people who don't have big ears, buying the meal that I should be cooking for Thanksgiving.

Tina sat back down with a thump with Jeremy following suit. The direction of Carol's gaze now allowed her to only see Tina's knee: a thick stump wrapped in spandex.

Just as well, she thought. If I don't see her face, I definitely won't be taking it with me to the next world. And why hasn't anyone from 'the other side' ever come back and told us what to expect? A sign of misty writing on the bathroom mirror announcing, 'there is no hell' or a ghostly tap on the shoulder accompanied by a hoarse 'you relive only your best memories' or how about a dream where a dearly departed gives you a tour of where all they've actually been since they did depart?

Carol's thirst had faded, and she noticed this, along with an obstruction of her vision that veiled her eyes as if she were looking through mosquito netting.

Am I losing my eyesight? She wondered, blinking heavily. No! Let me see just once more, the sun melting in crimson over the lake on a calm summer's evening… or my friend, Shelley, busting out laughing when I imitate my dog…. or another autumn. I would love to see another autumn. Bright orange, stunning yellow leaves with the sun shining off them by the lake. Oh…the lake! I always go back there. My haven. I should be dying there. If only I could tell my self-centered brother and sister that's where I want to go now. They never got it that the lake was always my favorite place. Some people can't see even when their eyes are working.

But I can feel it. Yes! I'm sensing the cool liquid coming over my body. Are we fortunate enough to be transported when we die to the place where we were the happiest? Our spiritual memories expand to encompass our spiritual beings and become reality?

"I can't believe I did that," the nurse gasped in disgust.

She reached to set the overturned pitcher of water upright and bent over to start blotting the thin blanket wrapped around Carol's meager frame.

"Probably feels good," Jeremy commented, swiping his finger under his collar. "It's hot in here!"

It sunk into Carol what had just happened as the nurse dabbed away at her covering. All that is inconsequential now, Carol thought. For I see the brightness that I have been longing for. There is my pathway now…my new world where I am myself, for myself, and for no one else. Goodbye, Tina and Jeremy. Whatever time you have left in this world that I now leave, use it to manage your own business, not that of others.

Carol's senses were closed off then to the hospital room's environment. They journeyed forward toward any stimuli that might be coming from a pulsating grayness that was inundated with points of light. She could make out images appearing through the movement of gray matter. Scenes, people that looked familiar, but at such a distance, unrecognizable.

The nurse had her fingertips pressed to Carol's neck like a puppy claiming territory over a bone. Though she knew it was futile, for the sake of the family she barely touched her ear to Carol's chest.

"I hear nothing," she said turning her head toward Tina and Jeremy. "I'm afraid she's gone."

The nurse watched their faces for some reaction. She waited quite a while.

Tina let go a snort mingled with a choking sound, causing her to pinch her nose together and inhale half a sigh through her mouth. She looked at Jeremy, who was watching the television mounted above Tina's head.

"I think it's time we go down to the cafeteria," she proclaimed. Jeremy nodded and followed his remaining sister out of the room, leaving the nurse to do their mourning for them, if she chose to.

Images became clearer to Carol, and what she next saw was an epiphany to her. There was her mother, who had been dead now for three years. Standing next to her mother was her aunt, who had perished along with her mother in the car that was t-boned by a drunken teen.

"I knew I was right!" Carol whispered to herself. "We do meet those who have passed!"

She ran with open arms to where her mother was ...

"Carol!" her mother said loudly, allowing her daughter to hug her, breaking it off when it seemed to be lasting too long.

"You're here so soon? What happened?" she nearly demanded and then carried on as if an answer wasn't necessary. "You look like you're about ten! Now, why did you choose that age to revert to, Carol? That was always your pre-puberty fat stage."

She turned to Carol's aunt. "Gina, remember Carol trying to wear those midriff tops in the summer and her belly was always sticking out underneath the lace?"

Carol stood with her mouth open, wondering how to respond. Then she thought better of it, simply looking down. She discovered she was wearing a pink and orange paisley bathing suit.

"I'll tell you about it later!" she called to them as she ran away. She ran for her life: for her afterlife. It would be an afterlife all her own at the lake.

THE BATTLE FOR THE DISKS OF JOY
By Robert Mackey

The Sweet Treat One had landed on Draykcab. The crew had been there before. They knew the perils awaiting them. The wicked queen, creator of the disks of joy for one. The queen alone could foil the mission. Her hair, in and of itself, was enough to frighten off even the most experienced of pirates. It sat atop her head like a pile of tied up rats. She carried an unusually short wand with a concaved, oval head, that when deployed, sent any and all who tried to rob her of the highly sought-after disks running for his life.

If the hag queen weren't enough, there was always the horde of multi-colored, oddly shaped ghosts. They stick together in a tight knit group; practically impossible to penetrate their front lines. Get caught by one of the big ones? It could take the whole crew to free the captive. This task was certain to drain every ounce of energy from one's light saber and empty his ray gun. Should one be so fortunate as to break through the front lines, things got no better. Next, the rear lines. That's where the truly hideous, oddly shaped, and thoroughly creepy ghosts awaited a crew's attack. And one could always encounter the hell hounds or the hover craft manned by the fat ogre who garnered his power from some magical elixir he drank from brown bottles. Yes, a successful mission would take an extremely well planned and executed assault. That, and a lot of luck.

Captain Krid set the Sweet Treat One down inside the floating walls which encircled the lair of the wicked queen and her ogre bodyguard. The captain rose from his chair. Without looking at any of the crew, he stood before the screen. He stood in silence for, what seemed to the crew, an eternity.

They waited, frightened, anxious. The captain had gotten them through many battles. However, just because the team had never sustained a casualty, and no man was ever left behind, it didn't mean there would be no wounds, no long recovery time after the inevitable injuries which were almost certain to be incurred during the battle.

Staring at the screen, the captain finally spoke.

"One would never expect a place so beautiful could be so full of danger."

He stared out at the expanse of green, calm waters, the lush trees which floated, rooted magically, in the still sea. He shook his head. He turned to the crew.

"Well, we know what we have to do. We know the perils which most certainly await us. But as we're all aware; the disks are worth fighting for. And we know the joy they bring. While unbelievably intoxicating, their ability to induce happiness is very short-lived. Especially if we're caught."

The crew nodded their agreement. Except Belac. Belac was the latest addition to the well-seasoned crew. Belac had witnessed many missions, failures and successes. Though he always followed orders to the letter, he never went into battle with the same fearlessness as the rest of the crew.

Captain Krid addressed the troops. "To arms!"

Eibbor and the captain's number two man, Yllib, were up in a heartbeat, fastening their weapon belts around their waists. Belac took a little longer, and as usual needed the help of one of the other crew members to ensure he had his weapons situated properly. The captain smiled at the young recruit, knowing full well he would become an excellent warrior.

"So, light sabers fully charged? Ray guns set to kill?" asked the captain.

There were affirmative nods all around.

"Let's do this," said the captain.

As always, Captain Krid was the first down the ship's emergency escape pole. He was followed immediately by Yllib and Eibbor. Belac took the ladder to the water's surface.

The crew crouched at the foot of their ship in their specialized boots which allowed them to walk on water. Krid gave the attack order. With battle cries of AHHG! filling the warm, sundrenched confines of the witch's lair, the crew headed straight for the almost ever-present ghosts. They went straight for the huge, white ones first. Swords slashed at the enemy, the first of which fell from the air, landing atop Belac.

It consumed the young recruit. His three comrades in arms came to his rescue, slashing at the wicked apparition and firing bursts from their ray guns into the fiend. Within seconds the crew had taken out the ghost and freed the young Belak from its clutches. There were three more of the large, white devils. They too were slashed and shot to pieces.

Eibbor cried, "I'm out!"

Yllib stated the same thing.

"Fall back and reload," cried the captain.

The pirates huddled between the fore legs of their floating ship, frantically reloading the pods which the ray guns fire.

The captain, before giving the order to resume the attack, said, "I know the small, colored, hideous ghosts have never posed much of a threat, but they have to be taken out."

Yllib and Eibbor nodded their agreement to the order. Belac's head dropped. But he stood, his ray gun in one hand, light saber in the other. He readied himself for the carnage he was about to commit.

The crew ran toward the enemy. Battle cries were once again employed. They hit the second string of the hag's defenses. Sabers swung wildly. The hideous, menacing ghosts fell from where they hovered high above the crew's heads. The pirates beat the disgusting things into the sea, ensuring they wouldn't be sneaking up behind them as the onslaught continued. And then it happened, as if cued by a movie director. The water dogs appeared. The appendage at the back of their bodies swung wildly from side to side. They approached the crew fearlessly. Ray guns fired repeatedly and just a few slashes of the pirate's sabers sent the beasts retreating from the battlefield.

The lions lay still, curled up on the throne which the ogre was known to occupy. The captain gave the order to take them out. The lions were hit by number of ray gun blasts. One ran up a tree. The other found shelter under the structure which supported the ogre's chair.

Belac cried out, "I'm out of ammo!"

The rest of the crew checked their guns. They too were dangerously low on pods.

The captain, once again, yelled, "Fall back!"

Under the ship, the captain assessed the situation. "We're looking good. Almost there."

The disks were already in place on the shelf where the crew knew they would find them.

The captain addressed the troops. "Everything is going according to plan. We've taken out the ghosts. The water hounds have taken to hiding, as have the lions. When we go in for the disks, be sure to avoid the tree where the one lion is." He spoke his last order directly to Belac. "That lion could leap from the tree, and that would be the end of you. It's your job to watch our six. The other positive is that the ogre is nowhere to be seen. So, we go straight for the disks. We don't need them all. One will be enough for all of us. Everybody ready?"

Salutes came from both Eibbor and Yllib. Belac, feeling good about how things were progressing, gave an emphatic nod.

No sooner than Captain Krid said "Let's finish this mission," the sliding door to the hag's lair slid open. The Ogre stepped out onto the floating deck where his throne sat. He had two of the brown bottles which held the magical elixir. He took his seat, taking in sight of the lifeless bodies of the ghosts as they floated on the sea's surface. He shook his head and drank of his elixir.

The captain held up a hand, indicating the troops should hold their position.

"Shit. Everything was going so well. We're gonna have to take him out. Is everyone fully loaded? He won't go quietly."

Affirming nods came from the crew. Belac narrowed his eyes, checked his gun, and said, "Let's get the fat bastard."

The captain looked to Belac, a broad smile stretched across his face. "Now you're getting it! Okay everyone. One more obstacle. We take out the ogre and head straight for the disks. Ready? Charge!"

Battle cries were screamed. Belac charged forth, ahead of the rest of the crew. He was not to be denied his spoils.

The ogre sat upon his throne as if he were the king of the realm. His fat belly lay on the thighs of his enormous legs. He didn't flinch as the crew of the Sweet Treat One approached at a dead run. Within six feet of the ogre, ray guns were exhausted of pods. The crew didn't even slow their attack. Belac was the first to reach the ogre. He slashed madly at the legs of the huge creature. He was joined just a second later by the rest of the crew. They too sliced away at the ogre with their light sabers. He screamed cries of pain, repeatedly pleading for the pirates to cease their brutal attack. The crew was relentless. Blows fell on every exposed inch of the giant's flesh. Their booty was just steps away. They would not be denied.

The ogre abandoned his throne. He fell to one knee. He righted himself, heading for the safety of the hag and her home. He had dropped one of his bottles of elixir and had left the other behind as he ran for the sliding door of the hag's lair. Safely behind the glass door, he pointed a fat index finger at the pirates and then shook his fist furiously. Oddly, he was smiling.

The captain ordered Belac to watch his six. He told Yllib and Eibbor to take up positions on either side of the shelf where the disks rested. Everyone nodded their acknowledgement of the captain's final orders, in what was, thus far, a very successful mission.

The captain headed straight for the disks as Yllib and Eibbor flanked him to either side. Krid sat crouched under the shelf as his protectors leaned up against the exterior of the Hag's lair. He nodded to Yllib and Eibbor. They returned his nods, smiling hopefully. The prize they fought so valiantly for lay within an arm's reach of the captain.

Krid reached up. He had a hand on one of the disks. As he slid it toward the edge of the shelf, the wand of the wicked hag came down hard on his knuckles. With a yelp, he withdrew his hand and stood fully erect. The hag was nowhere to be seen. He reached again for the disk.

Just as he attempted to abscond with it, the hag slid the glass door open hard. It crashed into the frame which held it and bounced back toward her. She slid it out of her way and burst onto the structure which supported the fat ogre's throne. She screamed that unbearable, high-pitched scream that to the crew meant, the op was a failure.

The hag was on the three pirates in a heartbeat. Eibbor, who was nearest the glass door, took a blow from the wand to the side of his head. Krid caught a hit to his shoulder and one directly to his right ear. Yllib ran for his life. Belac had been backing slowly away from the scene ever since the ogre stood in front of the glass door, shaking his fist at the entire crew, knowing full-well, nothing good was going to come of the mission.

The hag yelled at the retreating crew, "Dirk, Billy, Robbie, Caleb! How many times have I told you? The pies have to cool!"

She surveyed the carnage which lay before her. "You little hellions! What the hell have you done to my laundry? You will pick up every piece of laundry in this yard! You will fold it! You will put it all away. And if you've damaged even one of my bras you won't be able to sit for a week!" She hesitated for a moment, then continued: "And I want all of those nerf darts off the lawn! Your father will be mowing soon. And get every single dish out of that tree house and get your butts in here. You all have a good, sound beating coming from my spoon!"

Caleb had retreated behind a bush against the backyard fence. The other three boys walked slowly toward the tree house, dejectedly dragging their plastic swords through the too tall grass.

Their mother yelled after them.

"And get yourselves washed up for dinner. And there will be no pie for any of you for dessert!"

A resounding 'aw, mom' came from three of the beaten pirates. Caleb probably wouldn't be seen or heard from for hours.

THE NO. 6 CLUB

By Alec Sillifant

6706428 woke with a starter motor from a 1976 Ford Capri resting on his naked chest. The protruding ribs seem to cradle the mechanical lump like the delicate crown that grips the diamond of an engagement ring.

"It's about time you got this autoeroticism under control."

6706428 sat bolt upright in his bed. "Mum! What are you doing in my room?"

"A man of your age…playing with car parts. You've always been a strange one."

"How could I be anything else with a mother who's pyronoid?"

"Just because I'm pyronoid doesn't mean they're not out to set me on fire."

The mother and son stared in angry silence for a moment before the woman's face softened.

"What's the matter with you, 6706428? You can tell me, I'm your mother."

6706428 placed the starter motor on his bedside cabinet, next to the spark plug from a BSA Bantam, a bonnet ornament from a Mark II Jag, a tub of hand cream and an empty tissue box. He sighed as he had done many times before.

"Why can't I have a name; a real name made of letters. What would be so-"

"Oh, not this again. We've been through this over and over since you were a little boy," said 6706428's mother, plonking herself on her son's bed. "It's the law and more than that, the world is a better place for the lack of names. Do you think everything was lovely when the likes of Adolf Hitler, Joseph Stalin, and Paul McCartney were kicking about? It was proven by the Royal High Numerologist decades ago that names were evil and anyone who had a name, which was everyone, held the potential darkness within them."

"Really, you're buying the High Numerologist BS? I heard it was a move by Facebook to make everyone easier to catalogue for targeted adverts," said 6706428.

"And now you're adding conspiracy theorist to your fender polishing tendencies, brilliant. I sometimes wonder if you're my son at all."

"And if all names are bad, why am I allowed to call you Mum?"

"That's not a name, it's a title. Titles are labels of trust, like Doctor or Nurse, Holy Father or Lawyer…maybe not so much the last two. I call you son, don't I?"

"It's not the same," said 6706428, shaking his head, "I don't feel like it's…me."

6706428's mother sighed her defeat and rose from the bed.

"You're going to be late for work. And get a shower, there's oil on your chest."

6706428 threw back the covers and walked toward the bathroom.

"And make sure there's no matches in the house before you leave, will you?"

"Yes, mum."

6706428's day in the call centre dragged as always but it was lightened slightly when he received a call from 768 complaining about their gas supply. He felt almost honoured to speaking to someone so old…or at least he did until the laboured breathing on the other end of the line stopped mid-gripe. As 6706428 hung up, he wondered if the call had been recorded for training purposes or posterity.

The bus journey home offered the usual, standing room only, sardine luxury and it took some self-control for 6706428 not to imagine the days when this vehicle would have been powered by a sexy 7.3 litre V8 diesel unit instead of the cold-hearted electric motor that silently hauled the collection of cramped bodies to destinations varied. As the terminus drew closer the carriage emptied, and he grabbed a seat to travel in comfort for the last few hundred yards to his stop. A white triangle, peeking from between the frame of his newly acquired perch and the coachwork, caught 6706428's attention and without thinking, he pinched it between forefinger and thumb and pulled. The business card that emerged was very basic; plain white background with a clear black font spelling out two lines of text:

'The No 6 Club' and beneath that, 'My name is Patrick McGoham'.

6706428's heart was beating hard, and he was struggling for breath; just like 768 had been only hours before. 'My name is Patrick McGoham'. The words echoed about his head. 'My name is Patrick McGoham…my name is…my name…my *name*.'

6706428 studied the card for any clues as to its origin. There was no address for The No 6 Club, nor Patrick

McGoham, on the card. No additional information at all. 'It's a hoax,' thought 6706428, 'a schoolkid's prank, knocked up in IT class.'

He flipped the card back and forth in some vein hope the movement would trigger a clever mechanism that would give up the missing data, but nothing of the sort happened. Wracking his brains for possible answers, 6706428 began tapping the card against the tip of his nose, gazing into space, his mind whirring with possibilities.

The smell came faint at first, like the merest hint of roses in cheap fabric conditioner, but with each tap it grew and took hold in his hippocampus. 6706428 smiled.

'I know that scent and I know there's only one place in the city I've smelt it before.' He shot out his hand and pressed the button that goes 'ding' to let the bus driver know you want to get off at the next stop. Today it had an even sweeter tone than ever before. It was a bell that tolled a promise of a brighter future.

'Vintage and Collectable Auto Parts Inc.', despite its flash name, was little more than an old school breakers yard with the famous '5-5' warrantee system (five minutes or five yards) that catered to a very small, and rich, clientele running classic vehicles. 6706428 was familiar with the company, as he'd been chased off the site many times for having far too much of an *unhealthy interest* in some of the half-stripped, fossil fuel cars of the past.

By the time he'd arrived, due to the walk/trot from the bus stop, it was 6pm and the establishment's gates were chained closed with a heavy-duty padlock, but you don't get easily defeated by a ten-foot wire fence when you're a dedicated auto-erotic.

Climbing down a teetering tower of Toyotas on the far side of the fence, whilst also fighting to keep his carnal urges in check, 6706428 landed on the muddy lot and stealthily made his way to within sight of the porta-cabin at the centre of the columns of twisted vehicular metal. A single bulb burned in the wire framed bulkhead lamp above the external door of this central hub but the interior of the cabin, viewed through a single glass panel, was in unyielding darkness.

6706428, with laboured breath, sprinted to the entrance and, to his surprise, found the door unlocked and more than willing to his advances. He stepped inside. The office was nothing special. A desk, a PC, a couple of chairs, and a filing cabinet. A filing cabinet that wasn't completely flush to the wall.

'Can a filing cabinet, like the old door joke, be ajar?' thought 6706428. Steeling himself he crept forward and peered around the metallic faced column of drawers, behind which was an opening, no more than twenty inches across, that revealed a set of descending stairs. 6706428 swallowed.

'You've come this far.'

He squeezed through the gap and began to descend.

At the bottom of the steps was a room no bigger than five yards by five yards square, subtly lit by Edison bulbs in numerous wall fittings and a collection of the same zigzagging filaments glowed from the points of an impressive central ceiling chandelier, fashioned from a wooden cartwheel. An impressive oak bar, adorned with ceramic beer pumps, ran the length of the back wall and a scattering of amply padded leather seats gathered, like wildlife at a watering hole, atop of a thickly woven Axminster. The 19th century had been funnelled in neat to warm the cockles of this cold basement's heart.

Around thirty people populated this secret den of opulence, laughing and talking, completely ignorant of the trespasser at the foot of the steps. 6706428 marvelled at the sight before him but more than that he revelled in the sound of names being used with carless and regular abandon. He smiled broadly, as if he had got his hands on a very rare 1953 Morris Minor headlight with original glass lens.

One by one conversations rolled to a stop as the group in growing numbers noticed the grinning interloper standing and staring at them as if they were enthralling exhibits in a museum of automaton. Soon, silence was the only sound. One man, dressed in an oily overall, peeled himself from the muted group and approached 6706428 before making obvious efforts to keep a prudent distance.

"Can I help you, sir? Our offices are closed for the day."

6706428's smile broadened. "Do it again."

"Do what again?"

"Say your names."

The man gave a friendly chuckle. "You must be mistaken, we weren't using names; we were using our officially ordained numbers, as required by law."

"No, I heard you," said 6706428, "I know I did."

"Sometimes if you say a number, it might sound like a name," said the man, taking two paces forward to place a reassuring hand on 6706428's shoulder. "Take number one, it could sound like Bon; or two could be misheard as...Lou. Three could easily be misconstrued as..."

The man scratched his head as if forgetting the lines from a not-so-diligently rehearsed monologue.

"Ste!" offered a helpful voice in the crowd.

"Yes, Mick, what do you want?" came a less-than-helpful reply from the other side of the room.

"Ha!" said 6706428, pointing an accusing and triumphant index finger. "I knew it."

The man, his hand still resting on 6706428's shoulder, scowled into the group who all looked suitably sheepish in response.

"Listen, it's not what it looks like," he said, his attention returning to the unwelcome visitor, "it's just a few colleagues getting together for a quiet drink after work and using their official numbers in a perfectly legal way."

"Then how do you explain this?" said 6706428, producing the business card he'd found on the bus.

The man took the card and looked at it for a few seconds before blowing a huge breath of exasperation out.

"Paddy. Care to explain this?" He held up the business card for all to see.

A stout man dressed in tweed jacket and kilt and sporting an impressive waist length double plaited beard turned his face down to study his tan brogues. He muttered like a chastised child.

"What was that?"

Paddy muttered a little louder but still incomprehensibly.

The man with the business card held aloft removed his other hand from 6706428's shoulder to stand front and centre of the group.

"Everyone. The first rule of The Number Six Club is…"

"No personalised stationery," came the choral reply.

"Exactly." The card holder let that sink in for a second before speaking again. "The *second* rule of The Number Six Club is…"

"No personal-"

"Actually, no, I'm changing that," said the man shaking his head. "Henceforth the second rule will be don't forget to make sure the bloody secret door is closed *and* locked."

The group mumbled and nodded their agreement.

"I'm keeping this too, Paddy," said the man, pocketing the business card. "It's got a date with the shredder."

Paddy rubbed at his beard, muttering once more.

"Something to say?"

Paddy shook his head and by default his beard.

"I didn't think so," said the man, before turning back to face 6706428. "Okay, it looks like you've busted us. What are you, government official? Rozzer?"

"Neither," said 6706428.

"So, it's blackmail then, is it?" said the man, doing little to hide the contempt in his voice. "You do realise it's all of us against the one of you?"

The rest of the group mumbled to illustrate the mathematical ratio was indeed correct but possibly not quite as threatening as suggested.

"Things could get nasty for you."

"No, not at all," said 6706428, "the complete opposite actually."

"You want us to blackmail you?" said a tall woman, gesticulating with the glass of brandy in her hand, getting a droplet of it on her pink twinset in the process.

"Okay, maybe not the complete opposite. I…" 6706428 paused for dramatic effect, "want to join you. I want a name too."

There was a lot of hushed conversations, but all were of the idea that this was not a good idea.

"I'm not sure about this," said Paddy, "it's not that easy to get into The No 6 Club. It's very exclusive. There's rules and stuff."

"Like the rules about personalised stationery and keeping the door locked, Paddy?" said 6706428, with a tad more venom than he intended.

The man in the boiler suit rubbed his chin. "Good point, the statutes are a little...in flux at present." He turned to face his fellow members. "What do you say, friends, shall we add another name to the revered register of epithets?"

Their answer was little more than a muted shuffling of indecisive feet.

"I'll put it this way. Shall we let this man join us or are we prepared to risk having our secret club exposed to the nameless numbers out there, some of whom can be a little touchy about this kind of thing?"

The group got down to some intense mumbling.

"So, are we going to let him join us?"

The subterranean room echoed with a resounding "Aye!"

The man extended a grubby hand from his oily sleeve and 6706428 took it.

"Welcome to The No 6 Club, I'm Spartacus."

"No, I'm Spartacus!" shouted a voice from the group.

"And that's Bozo," said Spartacus, "he fancies himself as the club's clown."

"This is so exciting," said 6706428, "I've dreamt of this for years."

"I know what you mean, everyone here understands what it's like to make claim to a moniker of your own. Talking of which, would you like us to assign you a name or have you got one in mind?"

6706428 smiled. "Oh, I know what I want to be called alright."

"Excellent," said Spartacus, then he called for the attention of all. "Friends! Friends! Our newest member is about to own his own identity, so as is traditional we shall all witness this rebirth of a named man. Go ahead, my friend, denumerise and christen yourself anew for all to hear."

6706428 cleared his throat. He was smiling so broadly it was on the verge of painful.

"I…my name…my name…is…Clint Eastwood."

The group stayed silent. Spartacus whispered in 6706428's ear, "are you sure? it has subtle and ironic undertones that may not be realised by all, don't you think?"

"My name is Clint Eastwood," said Clint, with a stern finality.

"Fair enough," said Spartacus, "I won't laugh at your mule. Ladies and Gentlemen, I give you-"

The stairs leading into the club thundered with the sound of heavy footsteps barrelling at speed down them. Launching himself into The No 6 Club headquarters a man, wearing 13th century leather armour over crimson silks, waved a vicious-looking polearm to carve patterns into the air before him that suggested very brutal intent.

"Oh shit," said Spartacus, "it's Genghis. How did he find our new premises?" Then he noticed the business card tucked into the sash tied about the man's waist. "Paddy!"

The No 6 Club membership began to scatter in all directions, smashing cut crystal and spilling claret with panicked abandon. Within the confining area of the basement, they looked akin to the proverbial headless chickens that in a sad truism they were about to resemble even more closely.

Clint turned to face the raving warrior warlord and hoping to say something to cool the invader's ire, and on some level also hoping to become the hero of the club and thus a valued asset to it, opened his mouth.

"My name's Clin-"

As the steel of Genghis' blade pierced his midriff fully through, splitting intestines and shattering spinal column, Clint's final thoughts involuntarily focussed on his mum. The fact occurred to him that maybe his mum had been right.

Maybe there was some dark and malevolent power in certain names after all.

'Maybe I should have been content as a number. Maybe I should try to resist getting turned on by automobile parts.'

Then he thought his final, enlightening thought.

'Maybe...maybe I should have chosen to call myself...Indestructo Man...'

SILICONE THERAPY:

KEEPING ABREAST OF NEW DEVELOPMENTS

By E.L. Bonlien and J. Gnolhcs

Baltimore Research Facility

(Story By Neil Nobleand Jackson Schlong)

The current controversy over silicone treatment has reached such voluminous proportions, that a more sober and scholarly review of the problem is needed in all of its sociocultural, ethnic, scientific and economic aspects.

Historically, the credit for the discovery and application of Bustular Mechanics belongs to Dr. Orville A. Whopperknocker. His pioneering work, which involved both vector analysis and magnitude appreciation, culminated in the now famous, mathematical formula for computing breast enlargement as a function of the amount and number of silicone injections.[1] His work, gained him considerable medical praise and numerous scientific honors. Some of these were the Amazon Award, the D. Parton Memorial Award and the Booby Prize. Dr. Whopperknocker was also the first

President and founder of the Best Advancement of Breast Enhancement Society or **BABES**. The learned journal as well as its official organ is **The Bosom**.

While the argument over the pros and cons of 'realities' rages on, a more dispassionate appraisal of the magnitude of the problem, statistically speaking, becomes necessary. The U.S. government's authoritative 100-page report[2] reveals that, at least, 33% of all American women suffer from substandard endowments. Other figures from this report are equally depressing. The problem does appear to be limited to women who belong to the Caucasian race. Of course, there will always be exceptions. In lay terms, for Caucasian women we reference these cases as the 'Dolly Dilemma'. For women of color, who generally do not require enhancement but do suffer from the same substandard endowments, we use the 'Ross Inverted Growth Structure' terminology. Concern with the problem has even been included in literature.[3]

The growing use of silicone treatments and the continued rising demand anticipated for them has given rise to several learned economic treatises dealing with the problem.[456] There has also been commentary from acute social observation.[7] Moreover, the widespread use of silicone treatments on college campuses has created a similar rising concern among educators.[89]

There is an additional concern over the inflated use of silicone and the redirection of natural resources. The Waverly Obfuscation Paint Preservation Entitlement and Restoration Society (WOPPERS) has taken umbrage to the reckless use of silicone for breast enhancement.

Paint has already become a low priority because of the ever-increasing call for silicone in the healthcare and aviation industries. They claim that the now compromised manufacturing of silicone, for its use in paint stability, is no longer readily available. A recent article by B.G. Titsabound makes the argument that the future health of Americans will better off using silicone inside detection machinery rather than woman's breasts.[10] The aviation industry has already established its claim on silicone by arguing that it serves to prop up other deflated and otherwise sagging systems.[11]

Chemical means of breast enlargement continues to be a rapidly expanding area. Progress has been somewhat marred by the occasional overtreatment of zealous, but inexperienced practitioners, with resulting gross over enlargement of the breasts and related iatrogenic complications of considerable dimensions. Such cases have recently reached alarming proportions. We have redesignated our efforts at remedial treatment by referring to this as supportive therapy. The design of corrective devices, which are both prosthetic and aesthetic, has created a new cosmetic specialty in brassiere architecture.

The problem seems to have been not without precedent among the ancients. Biblical experts have reminded us of the quote, "Her cups runneth over." The leading authorities in the field attended a recent conference on ethics. They created a national set of standards for adequate housing and made provisions for the prosecution of violators found guilty of non-support. An accompanying manual provides technical recommendations for manufacturers trying to cope with the problem.[12] Its basis is a previous classic publication in a related area.[13]

The most primitive attempt, in this direction, was a feminine adaptation of the medieval breastplate. This was not without its disadvantages. Excessive weight was responsible for several cases of shoulder separation. An obsolete ventilation system, for perspiration evaporation, also proved unequal to the task. The resulting rust deposits on the interior of the cups were a perennial source of complaints.

It also created considerable difficulty for breastfeeding mothers. More than one infant reportedly shattered an entire set of milk teeth during sudden hunger pangs. Corollary advantages do include a drastically shorter time required for weaning. In addition, the company manufacturing this model appears to have gone bust. More recent design innovations have since become available. Some are employing flying buttresses and principles borrowed from cantilever construction. Models that are more sophisticated will blow up the market as they continue to expand.

Lastly, a word on the etymology of 'silicone.' While it is somewhat obscured, it is believed, by some authoritative pedantologists, to be derived from the Latin 'valde magna pectora,' which can be translated as 'silhouetted with meat' or possibly 'copious cones.'

Further observation, investigation, discussion along with due diligence will be ongoing for quite some time to come.

FOOTNOTES

1. Whopperknocker, Dr. O.A. "Growth Curves and the Inflation Index". Medicus Astronomicus,

1985, VIII, pp. 71-89.

2. Sam, Uncle "Making Mountains out of Molehills". U.S. Government Report No. T-372435.

3. Shakespeare, William. Much Ado About Nothing. A tragedy in two parts. Paucity Press, London, 1599.

4. Jones, B.A. "Recessions and What to do About Them". Journal of Esoteric Economics, 1987,

XXVIII, pp. 22-26.

5. Whopperknocker, Dr. O.A. "The Contribution of Silicone to the Gross National Product".

Journal of Medical Microeconomics, 1986, VIII, pp. 213-218.

6. Jones, B.A. "The Pros and Cons of Subsidation to Depressed Areas". Journal of Medical

Microeconomics, 1988, XIII, pp. 41-45.

7. Wolf, I.M. "Growing Areas of National Attention". Girlwatchers Almanac, 1988, IV,

pp. 36-44. Reprinted by Dr. O.A. Whopperknocker (ed.) Helping Your Bosom Blossom,

Poverty Press, 1988, pp. 69-269.

8. Smith, J.A. "Building a Better Student Body". Journal of Educational Reform, 1989, in Two Volumes.

9. Smith, J.A. "Inadequacies Beneath Female Student Uprisings". Journal of Psychosomatic Sophistries, 1989, XIII, pp. 313-325.

10. Titsabound, B.G. "Healthcare Outlooks on the Evolving Recovery Syllogism". The Journal of Duplicity, 1990. pp. 34-49.

11. Conversation with Maye I. Holdem, former President (1982-1992) of the Association of Proud Aviators in Retirement, 1991.

12. Johnson, M.E. "Expansion Engineering and the Agony-Relief Ratio". BOSOM Companion Monographs, 1992, pp. 3-5.

13. Siem, C.E. "Stress Analysis of the Strapless Evening Gown". The Indicator, November 1986, p. 54.

THE NAMIB KING – A SURVIVAL STORY
By Mason Bushell

It was the burning in his nostrils that shocked him to consciousness.

Aviation fuel.

He coughed his throat clear of sand and felt his stomach plummet.

Land and sky flipped in his mind.

The desert yawned toward the cockpit.

Darkness.

"Aww, shit. I crashed."

Kwami winced as he rolled his face out of the sand. He was instantly blinded by the intense sun cooking him as if he'd landed on a chargrill. Every blink revealed more of the disaster around him.

Small fires crackled from the remains of his Cessna Grand Caravan. The safari plane had been a reliable old girl, taking 12 tourists to see the Namibian Skeleton Coast every day.

Now, she was twisted wreckage strewn across the desert.

What had gone so drastically wrong?

Kwami sat in the sand, feeling pain in every part of his anatomy. He'd been flying South to the Arandis Airfield for routine maintenance on the aircraft. Something he'd done regularly.

Eyes closed, Kwami remembered the Cessna lurching skyward. A sudden uplift, and then the sand arrived. A swirling storm of desert dust assaulted every vent and window on the aircraft until the engine suffocated and the end arrived.

Kwami gained his feet. A knee injury burned as it struggled with his weight. Running his arm over his chest revealed a cracked rib. He looked at his safari shirt and shorts, bloodstained from many wounds to his limbs, face and stinging, broken nose.

"Why am I still alive? You still planning to punish me, Fate?" he grumbled while gazing around him.

He'd been fortunate in this hellish landscape. The plane had landed on the white sand of an ancient riverbed. The red dunes of the Namib Desert stretched into endless blue skies in every direction. A few long-dead tree trunks stuck out like morbid black skeletons in the dry and dead landscape.

"You want to kill me slowly? Let's play!"

Kwami found his supply pack in the wreckage, drank a little water, and despite pain wracking his knee, he walked into the desert.

Kwami was no soldier; he was just defiant.

The 35-degree centigrade heat of the relentless sun beat upon him with no mercy as he ascended one dune after another.

With a mile of mountainous sand behind him, he fell to his knees, chest heaving, drenched in sweat that glistened upon his baked skin, caked with blood. Atop a rusty dune carved into a wave by the harsh winds, he gathered his breath.

"You … will not … beat me!" he panted.

He poured the last few drops of water from his canteen into his mouth. It did nothing to satisfy his thirst as it stung his cracked lips.

"I refuse to be another skeleton in your macabre collection."

Kwami rose with a stagger. The dunes seemed to swirl in his vision. Dehydration was taking hold; he could feel it in his lowering blood pressure.

He took a step, slipped and fell. A yelp escaped his parched lips as he tumbled two hundred meters to the base of the dune.

"Oh, Namib, you're a cruel witch."

Kwami had landed limbs akimbo, face to the sky. He coughed sand from his lungs and rolled to his knees.

A low rumbling growl that rattled ribs answered his movement.

Kwami froze, eye to eye with a fearsome cat. He knew she was a rare Namibian desert lioness. A subspecies that'd learned to survive in this, the harshest environment on Earth aside from the Antarctic tundra. She didn't need water; the blood of a gemsbok, ostrich or Skeleton Coast seal would satiate her.

The golden lioness lowered her head, stretching her front legs. She made a puffing noise, then glanced behind her.

"Hello, Princess," Kwami raised a stalling hand.

Futile against such a powerful beast. She'd snap it off to reach him in a heartbeat. He spoke in reverence. The only way to respect the queen of the beasts.

"Please forgive my intrusion into your home."

The lioness glanced behind her once more.

He regained his feet. "I'm not dead yet. You need something, Princess?"

She turned away, retracing her paw prints in the hot sand.

Kwami nodded. "Very well, I will follow you."

In that moment, intrigue and wonder masked his injuries, allowing him to trudge onward.

The lioness glanced at the human many times as she trekked through the baking landscape.

Where was her pride? The king of the lions had to be nearby, and yet she was alone. Kwami followed her between the dunes. What he saw caused the breath to catch in his lungs.

Water glinted in the sunlight. A pond in a sea of sand. A life-giving watering hole in the driest hell on Earth. A wary, yet magnificent Gemsbok was drinking from the far side. His long, straight horns were menacing as he raised his black and brown head to the sky for a moment.

"Thank you for saving me, Princess."

She let out a rumble, a puffing note, then strode away.

Kwami fell to his knees at the waterside and drank for a long moment. The water was beyond tepid; it was hot, and yet it was delicious.

Princess was back; this time, she dropped something a few feet away with a sad-sounding grunt. She nodded toward it, then retreated into the shade of the dunes.

Kwami felt his eyes prickle. He was too dehydrated to create tears and yet felt the pang.

"I understand now."

He rose from the waterside and approached the bundle of fur in the sand. A beautiful lion cub. Princess had saved the human, now she was asking him to return the favor.

Princess grunted again.

"I will do all I can, I promise."

Kwami scooped the cub into his arms. He could feel no heartbeat. No rise and fall of the creature's chest. On his knees, he began massaging, pumping the cub's chest.

"Come on, little one!" Kwami cupped his little mouth and blew air into his lungs.

This little ball of fur would become the king of beasts, should he live. The most remarkable thing to behold.

Kwami continued to massage the cub, desperate to hear it breathe again.

A terrifying roar seemed to shake the desert.

The shadow of a mighty lion darkened the sand. He stood atop the dune, roaring into the sky! His mane was dark; his face scarred from terrifying battles for dominance. This was the ruler of the Namib Desert.

Princess leapt to her feet, putting herself between the human and the king. She roared back, her tones snarling with displeasure.

"Don't kill me, your majesty. I'm just trying to help," Kwami whispered before giving the cub another life-saving breath.

The lion took a mighty step toward the waterhole.

Princess roared again, warning him.

The lion charged her.

In Kwami's arms, the lion cub shuddered, it coughed and then gave a weak mew.

Princess switched from a defiant growl to a low hum, a happy note.

The lion stopped in a cloud of dust, mane whipping about his battle-drawn face. He gave a deep grunt.

The cub seemed to reply with a tiny mew.

Kwami scooped water into his little mouth as the lioness approached him. He looked between her and the lion on the dune.

The king of beasts seemed to nod his majestic head. He turned and strode away like a fearless warrior.

"That's twice you saved me, Princess," he said, presenting the cub to her.

She licked his little face, nuzzling him in a moment of ecstasy. A moment of motherliness that seemed unfitting for such a dangerous creature.

Kwami smiled at her, "I will leave you two in peace, Princess. Thanks again for the water and my life."

He filled his bottle in the watering hole and gazed upon mother and cub one last time.

She uttered a puffing sound and nodded her head to the West.

Kwami nodded and walked away. She'd let an item of prey escape in a place where sustenance was scarce. To stay here would be foolish; she would not give him a second chance when her cub cried for food.

Princess had one last gift in store. Her direction led Kwami to the Skeleton Coast. He arrived where the stormy Atlantic Ocean met the arid desert.

"Now, I have millions of gallons of water, and I cannot drink a drop," he said, while picking his way through the skeleton of a whale on the stony, rubbish-strewn beach.

Even here in this remote wilderness, the plastic, the detritus of human waste, blighted the landscape. Kwami kicked a broken stool and stepped into the surf.

A humming note reached his ears.

Was it the Jackal prowling the shoreline a distance away?

No, the white-capped waves would drown her voice.

Kwami sheltered his eyes with a hand. A glint of light in the sky. A helicopter drawing near. He waved his arms in a wide 'Y' shape. A signal for help.

The white helicopter roared overhead — had it seen him?

"Hey, down here!" Kwami yelled. Desperate for salvation.

The helicopter seemed to recede into the sky.

"No, don't go!"

It spun about above the waves and dropped onto the beach fifty meters away.

"Ahoy, there. Need a lift?" said the pilot.

"Albin, I'm glad to see you." Kwami hugged the man. A member of his safari team.

"When I heard your plane had vanished from radar. I began a search at once." Albin handed him a bottle of water.

Kwami drank every drop. "I can't thank you enough," he said as they entered the helicopter.

Albin lifted the craft into the sky and headed for home.

"I saw your crashed plane a while back. How'd you get this far without dehydrating?" he asked through his headset.

Kwami glanced toward the distant watering hole and smiled, "You wouldn't believe me if I told you."

Even as he spoke, he understood why fate had crashed his plane and let him survive. The Skeleton Coast had a newborn king, and Kwami was his savior.

CONFRONTATION ON A TRAIN
By Betty Mermelstein

We boarded the massive steel carrier on rails in the morning. I was awed by its size and obvious power as it had charged into the station. When I turned back again on the stairs to look out through the opened doors, a man was waving and smiling at me, while maintaining his position on the station platform. Even way before stranger danger, my five-year-old mind wasn't sure if this was right. I stared back at him before pivoting and following my family up the stairs and into the train car.

There he is again. I'm on the ascending steps of a train again, turning and looking behind me, but it's thirty-five years later, and I see him looking up at me from the platform. It's not the same man, but the memory becomes current like an arrow shooting forward through space. I hurry to board the car and huddle into a seat, turning toward the supposed protection of the seat back and window juncture.

As I comfort myself, I sigh, chastising myself for letting an old memory affect me in that way. I turn my attention to the front of the car where the man is now entering the train. He looks back and sees me. He smiles: a kind of knowing, smug grin, and enters, finding a seat several rows ahead of mine. Without another second, I stand and maneuver my way to the car behind me.

One half of an hour later, I decide to find the dining car. I sit, and after giving my order, I look up. The man is sitting at the table next to mine. How did he get there without my knowing? Perhaps when I was ordering and the waiter was blocking my view in that direction. I debate whether to stay or find the snack car.

Why, though? Is my paranoia shifting through my brain, causing waves of doubt that are cresting over my shore of confidence? Pushing aside my delusions that are causing prickles on my arms, I busy myself with the back of the menu that offers a history of the rail line, and I concentrate on how the inaugural train left the station in 1872 with 600 passengers ready to celebrate this newest…

"Excuse me, ma'am."

The waiter is trying to get my attention with a drink in his hand.

"This gentleman has paid for a drink for you: a scotch and soda," he states, nodding his head toward the table next to me, while placing the drink on the table. He then walked away.

I stare at the glass holding the caramel-colored liquid.

I glance at the man, who engages in a salutation to me by lifting his own glass. Hopefully, he can see my irritation at his gesture as I push away his unwanted gift. A large swig of water signals my preference of beverage as the waiter returns with my lunch.

I dive into my salad with confidence, though I fail to taste any of its contents. In trying to own my circumstances, I have lost the ability to absorb the surrounding positive aspects of my journey, having to concentrate instead on the current dilemma that I've been thrown into.

The salad is half-eaten and left abandoned on the table as I quickly rise and escape the dining car.

Choosing a seat in the last car on the train, I devise a plan. Not absolutely knowing what the next step might be for my pursuer, I calculate the possibility of opening the end car at the back and rolling out onto the track. After all, the use of cabooses went by the wayside in 1984, so I would just have to step around the replacement of a red lamp, let my body go limp, and slump over the side. Watching the scenery flash by at an unsettling rate causes me to question that plan.

Not again. It's a linear group of seating, easily available, and the 'gentleman' shows up in my group of seats.

I turn my attention back to the window and weigh the next possibility: an all-out confrontation. There are other people around us who would hear my accusation of him stalking me, witness to any of his retorts or threats he might make. This plan is shaping up to be a viable one, and I'm about to rise to stand my ground when I notice something out of the window. The train is slowing down to make another break in its forward progression, pulling into a station, and that station is the one before my destination.

All thoughts empty out of my head except for one: to get off the train now at this platform. It isn't far to the next one. I could take a ride-share car to where I need to be, where I could finally feel as safe as a bird in its nest. I rise, power ahead to the next car and the next, choosing an exit far enough from where I was just sitting.

Stepping off that car gives me a new appreciation for the crisp air I am now breathing in. It is filling me as a pure stream fills the forest floor.

I head to the main street, made evident by the line of restaurants and shops to my left. It's busy today with a gathering of shoppers and diners, families, couples, and singles. I've never been so euphoric being amid so many people with purpose.

Something catches my eye, causing me to look above the door of one of the eateries. On the doorframe is mounted an unexpected gargoyle. It's half-hidden, with a bandana tied around its head. I ponder this odd symbol and realize that this could be my protector. The gargoyle has long protected churches from evil, and this one showing up in my small-town realm is offering its watchful eye against my predicament on the train. It seems to me to be half-hidden so as to call my sole attention to its standing against the viciousness of the world. I am smugly content with my analysis of the matter and smile up at the medieval defender.

Something else causes my eye to scan downward, resting on an image in the restaurant window. It isn't something on the inside. It's a reflection from a form behind me. The figure is a man, smiling at me and stepping forward.

A FINE KETTLE OF FISH
By Robert Mackey

"I think I've got it, David."

"So, get another corpse to throw at the building across the street?"

"Or we could just stay here."

"So, why do we have to do this all the time?"

"For the umpteenth time David, we need to have the particle stream right. Or…"

"Oh, right. I remember. Or we splat into something or materialize in the middle of something solid."

"Now you're getting it."

"Perry?"

"Yeah, David?"

"So how many people have we…shot at the building?"

"Two hundred and forty."

"I thought you were supposed to be smart. Two hundred and forty tries seems... I don't know, like a lot."

"You try and build a teleporter from scratch with no help, no..."

"Hey! I help."

"I'm sorry, David. You are a big help. Now, go grab another corpse. And David?"

"Yeah, Perry?"

"You know what they say in the science world."

"What do they say Perry?"

"The two hundred and forty first time's a charm."

"Do they really say that, Perry?"

"No David. No, they don't. Corpse please."

Through the whole conversation, Perry had not once pulled his head from the access panel on the side of his invention. One last look at the settings and he closed the panel door as the squeaky wheels of the room service cart announced David's return.

David pushed the cart up beside the two bucket seats Perry had procured from one of the many abandoned cars in the street.

"Whew. He's a biggun'! What we gonna name him?" asked David.

"Your turn, isn't it?"

"Uumm. Beatrix!"

"He's a him."

"I was thinking, every other one we've named according to their sex. What if that's why the Move Us Over There Machine doesn't work?"

"See, David? You are much smarter than you give yourself credit for."

David beamed at his brother's compliment. The two wrestled the big, frozen, partially decomposed Beatrix into one of the car seats.

"Shall we?" asked Perry.

David saluted. "Case two hundred forty-one, Beatrix, ready for launch."

"Blast off," cried Perry, flipping the switch.

A one-inch beam of light shot through Beatrix. His body slowly folded into the stream like strawberries into a daiquiri. Beatrix had left the building. Perry and David ran to the front doors of the hotel. The horribly blood-and-gut-stained front of the bank across the street was not covered in a fresh coat of millions of tiny bits of human. Perry and David jumped up and down, spinning around as they hugged one another.

Perry stopped. He held David by the shoulders.

"If it worked, Beatrix should be in the middle of Eighty First Street."

The two tore out of the hotel and around the corner of the bank. Prior to rounding the corner onto Eighty First, Perry stopped. He waited for the trailing David to make up the few steps he'd fallen behind.

Grabbing David by the shoulders, Perry said, "Together."

"Together. On three," said David.

They counted aloud. "One, two, three!"

They jumped in unison out past the corner of the building. There, in the middle of Eighty First Street, sat Beatrix, looking no worse than he did sitting in the car seat just moments before.

The circular jumping up and down while screaming, "Aaahhh!" dance resumed.

David stopped the dance. "So, does this mean we're ready to go?"

"Ready as we'll ever be. Unless you want me to practice with you once to be sure?"

"You said we'd go together!"

"I'm just kidding, David. Of course we go together. I promised you a long time ago I would never leave you. Have I ever left you?"

"No."

"We are one, David."

"We are one, Perry."

The two put their foreheads together and nodded, something the brothers did whenever times were trying.

Walking back to the hotel, the burned-out buildings, cars, assorted rubbish, the decayed corpses of people and pets and birds and rats seemed not so depressing.

"You know, Perry? I'm gonna miss the hotel. It sure has been nice having a nice clean room every couple days…never having to make a bed or clean up after ourselves."

"That has been nice."

"So, where we going again?"

"A little place in the Pleiades."

"This place is nice, right?"

"David? You're looking for assurances. What do we know about assurances?"

David hung his head. "There aren't any."

"Right. We get in those car seats; it might be the last time we ever see each other. Or we stay here."

David looked up and down the street. Their surroundings took on that hopelessness that only the thought of escape could make even remotely bearable.

"We go. As planned. Together," said David.

David leaned his forehead towards his brother.

"Jonathan, I'm so sorry about Annie. So, now it's just you and me. What do you say we teleport off this dead rock before we join the rest of the deceased?"

Jonathan wiggled an antenna as a response. Zaytor was pretty sure the little cockroach couldn't understand him, but he figured the insect was probably on board with not starving to death like the balance of Xannax's population.

"I really tried to get the teleporter finished in time so a few others could join us. Gonna be kind of lonely with just you and me, but that's the way it goes. I mean, who knew all the water would just evaporate from one little meteor strike?"

Jonathan's antennas shook wildly.

"Please don't yell at me! I worked day and night!"

Jonathan took another bite of the head of his beloved.

"Annie isn't goanna sustain you for long and I am so weak that if we don't go soon, I'm not gonna have the energy to push the buttons."

Jonathan cocked his head, looking straight into Zaytor's eyes. The cockroach gave a little nod Zaytor could only take as an acceptance of the direness of their situation and his compliance to undertake the journey. Zaytor scooped up his little friend, pushed a few buttons, and jumped into the already operating particle beam.

It was a quiet day on Delphi 326. The azure sea lapped softly upon the sands of the beach. A soft breeze blew. Particle beams collided.

"Ow, shit!" cried Perry.

David yelled, "Ahhh, there's a bug on my face!"

The alien they crashed into sat rubbing his forehead.

"Um…Hi?" said Perry, as he stood nose to nose with the alien.

The alien proffered a tentacle. "Zaytor."

"Perry," said Perry shaking the alien's squishy tentacle.

"This is David."

Perry wiped his palm on his shirt even though there was nothing gooey or sticky, as he'd expected, from grasping Zaytor's limb.

Not knowing exactly how to approach the situation, Zaytor spoke forcefully, "Take me to your leader."

David reiterated, "Uh, hello? Bug on my face."

Zaytor removed Jonathan from David's face.

"This is Jonathan. He's my…travel buddy. So, your leader?"

Perry took in his immediate surroundings. Not seeing anyone or anything but a NO TRESPASSING sign, he said, "I'm the leader."

"You don't have a crown," said Zaytor flatly.

"Used to have one. Big cumbersome thing. Gave me neck problems."

"No matter. I haven't eaten in ages. I need to fall over and finish starving to death." Zaytor fell to his knees.

David pulled a Snickers bar from a pocket. After quickly unwrapping it, he handed it to Zaytor.

While Zaytor chewed and moaned ecstatically, Perry asked of David, "You brought food?"

"A little."

"Smart kid."

Zaytor spoke through a mouth of chocolate and peanutty nougat.

"That should keep me alive for another five minutes. Thank you so much."

David tore open a bag of Nacho cheese flavored Doritos and handed it to Zaytor.

"Where'd you get that stuff? We've been living off canned garbanzo beans and dolma leaves and spinach, and all the stuff people would rather die first than eat and you have Snickers and Doritos?" asked Perry.

"Well, when everyone lost their minds and started killing one another and looting, in all the mayhem, they overlooked the vending machines on the tenth floor."

"You've been hording this stuff…"

"I just found it yesterday! With the teleporter ready for another try, and getting Beatrix ready, the quick escape . . . I just forgot to tell you."

Perry reached into the bag of chips, pulled one out, and stuck it in his mouth.

"Wow. They traveled well. We could have brought more stuff."

Through a mouthful of chips, Zaytor said, "So, you just got here too."

Perry sat down, grabbed another chip.

"Yeah. I think our particle beams crashed into one another. May have been the only reason we stopped. What are the chances?"

Zaytor replied, "If you're talking about four particle beams from different galaxies colliding, I'd guess somewhere in the trillions to the trillionth power times one number less than infinity," he added, "So, I take it you escaped some apocalypse?"

"Yeah."

"You the only survivors?"

"Far as we know."

"What killed your planet?"

"Greedy people who wanted to control everything," said Perry.

"And you pretend to be king of this world as soon as you get here?" asked Zaytor.

Thinking hard and not finding the word he wanted, David asked, "What do you call that, Perry?"

"Ironic?" asked Zaytor.

"Typical?" guessed Perry.

"Either of those works," said David.

Perry looked around. "So, better try and find some food. What say we split up and have a look around? You two go that way and David and I'll go this way?"

"You're the leader," said Zaytor.

Walking along, Perry asked, "You notice how the water meets the sand in a perfectly straight line? No coves. No jutting peninsulas. Just perfectly straight."

David looked down the beach. Turning a hundred-eighty degrees, he looked back along the path they had travelled.

"Hmm. I'm guessing you'd consider that odd."

"Well. Yeah. Kind of."

"Perry, look! A humanoid!"

Looking up, and seeing the approaching figure, Perry said, "In case it's some kind of brain sucking alien, just…"

"Just what?" asked David, when it was clear Perry wasn't going to be finishing his thought.

"I don't know. Just don't pop the top off your head and offer him your brains like you did with the Snickers and Doritos."

David knitted his brow.

"C'mon. Stay close."

David fell in stride with Perry, mumbling, "Like what, I'm just gonna suddenly wander off?"

As the parties approached one another, David said, "That's Zaytor!"

"What? What makes you think that?"

"Look at his right tentacle. He's holding it palm up out in front of himself. He's carrying Jonathan."

"Yeah, that or the last bites of the brains of the last unsuspecting beachcomber he happened by."

"Oh, Perry."

A couple dozen steps later Perry said, "You're right!"

David beamed. He loved being right.

The parties met and Perry asked, "Well?"

"Nothing. Water on that side and nothing but sand as far as the eye can see."

David said, "Wait. You went one way. We went the other…"

"You are just on top of things today, Davey, my boy. He's right. We've been walking maybe…"

David checked his watch. "Twenty minutes."

"…Twenty minutes. I'm guessing we ambled along at about three miles an hour. That means this planet is only two miles in circumference."

"I'm not sure what a mile is, but I see your point. This is one small planet. How can it even have gravity?"

"It'd have to be super dense," said Perry.

Johnathan wiggled his antennae furiously.

"Be nice!" cried Zaytor.

"You understand him?"

"No. But I'm guessing he's saying I'm the densest thing here, having sent us to a tiny planet with no food."

"Maybe we should try inland, see if there's anything out there," said David.

"We'll need to determine if there's anything living in the sea that might be edible as well. Did anyone check if the water is fresh or salty?" asked Zaytor.

"Or if it's possibly sulfuric or hydrochloric acid?" said Perry.

"Or that," stated Zaytor.

Jonathan wiggled an antenna.

Perry said, "thanks Johnathan. You truly are the bravest of us."

Perry slapped the bottom of Zaytor's tentacle sending the cockroach into the water.

Zaytor screamed, "what are you doing?"

He scooped his little buddy out of the water.

"So, he okay?" asked Perry.

"Seems to be. You maniac!"

"And your wiggly flipper thing? Is it okay?"

Examining his appendage, Zaytor said, "Yeah, seems to be. You're still a maniac!"

"We had to know." Perry dipped the tip of a finger in the water and let it drop on his tongue.

"Not salty. So now we give it the old 'will it make us sick?' test." Perry scooped up a handful and slurped it up.

"Now, if I'm dead in a while, I would suggest not drinking the water. Shall we take Davey boy's suggestion and head back to where we landed, see if there's anything out there?"

Zaytor placed the end of his other tentacle over the one holding Johnathan, distanced himself a bit further from Perry, and said, "Yeah, sure."

"Well, that was fruitless," said Zaytor.

"Yup. Looks like we have half a planet of dandelions and half a planet of water, which seems to be potable," said Perry.

"And a no trespassing sign," said David. "Doesn't that bother anyone or, is it just me?"

Johnathan's antenna went wild, waving to and fro, forward and back. A hissing sound filled the air. Everyone turned in the direction Jonathan's still and rigid antenna now pointed. A green aura materialized at the water's edge, right next to the no trespassing sign. The green faded, replaced by a ten-foot-tall woman covered in scales, a pair of long, thick eyelashes fluttering above her reptilian eyes.

The creature looked from Perry to Zaytor to David and came to rest on Johnathan. Her tongue shot out at the speed of light, nabbed the cockroach, and returned him to her mouth. She chomped a couple times and swallowed poor Jonathan. She looked past the trespassers at the dandelion carpet beyond.

"Who the hell are you, why is my vacation home covered in dandelions, and do none of you know how to read?"

Zaytor stared into his empty hand. "You ate my friend."

"That answers none of my questions."

Perry said, "I'm Perry, this is David, my little brother, and the crying guy there is Zaytor. Jonathan, well, I guess he's no longer of consequence. I have no idea why your vacation home is infested with dandelions. They were here when we arrived. And we do know how to read but…"

"But? But what? If you know how to read, you certainly must realize you're not welcome here. That is unless your level of comprehension is somehow lacking."

"You ate my friend."

"I'll be eating you as well. But first you will eradicate this dandelion spurge you brought with you."

Perry lied, "Well, you just ate Jonathan. He could have eaten all your weeds in probably a couple, three days. We, on the other hand, might be good for about four to five plants a day each."

"Then I guess you probably ought to get busy," stated the snake lady flatly.

Another green sheen appeared. "Ah, there it is," said the snake.

The aura dissipated. In its place sat a little box no bigger than a loaf of bread. It was covered in buttons and toggle switches.

"What's that?" asked David.

"Well, my scrumptious looking little friend, that is a handy little device which I created to keep asteroids from colliding with my little Eden here."

"Eden?" asked Perry.

"It's a work in progress. So, get to munching. When I return, I expect to find this place free of those yellow flowering pests and the lot of you absent. Should I find you here…well let's just say it will be some time before I'll have the need to eat again."

"About that. You see, David and I come from…"

"Is this going to be a long story? Because frankly I'm not interested."

"I'll give you the condensed version."

The snaky woman blinked a protective cover down over her eyes, rolled them skyward, and crossed her arms over her chest.

"If you must."

"So, David and myself, we come from a planet destroyed by, well since this is the condensed version, it was destroyed. We are its sole survivors. Zaytor here comes from a planet which suffered the same fate. Johnathan, well, he was from Zator's planet as well. We both, Zaytor and I, managed to create a particle beam…"

The lizard lady let out a bored sigh.

"Let's just say, we have no way off your little Eden, hence the reason your sign was, well, not ignored exactly. We just aren't in the position to comply."

"If you built one particle, whatever, beam. I suggest you get busy and build another one."

Perry, Zator and even David searched their immediate surroundings and replied in harmony, "Out of what?"

Snake lady looked this way and that before replying:

"Let's see. You have dandelions, water, dirt, and a no trespassing sign. Should I find you here when I return, well, that's been addressed."

She was covered in a green sheen and was gone.

"Sooo…" said Perry, drawing the word out.

David, pointing off in the distance, said, "Guys?"

Perry and Zaytor turned.

"It's a meteor!" said Zaytor.

"Well, this is a fine kettle of fish," said Perry.

"You have a kettle of fish?" asked Zaytor.

"It's a saying."

"Meaning?"

"Meaning the situation we find ourselves in is less than desirable."

"Think maybe we ought to do something?" asked David.

Perry and Zaytor looked to the little box. Both dove for the contraption, Perry coming up with it. He pushed a button.

"Seems to have turned it to the left."

"Yeah," said David, "now it's coming right at us."

Zaytor started scribbling numbers in the sand.

"What are doing?" asked Perry.

"Calculating."

"But you have no idea how far away it is or how fast it's traveling."

"Calculated guess at best."

Perry and David watched Zaytor. After a minute Zaytor said: "A hair more to the left."

Perry tapped the same button he'd used before. "Like that much?"

"Can you find the button that moves it to the right in case my math is off a bit?"

Perry hit another button. The meteor sped up exponentially.

"Not that one!" cried Zaytor.

Perry was so shaken he dropped the box. It landed on what was the only rock any of the trio had seen on the tiny planet and broke into two, spewing out a heap of tangled wires.

"Ooops," mumbled Perry.

"Well, here it comes! If It's close enough jump on!" said Zaytor.

"And then?" asked Perry.

"And then at least we aren't snake food!"

"And we won't have to eat half a planet of dandelions," said David.

As the meteor grew nearer, its shape became more evident. It looked exactly like the head of an axe.

"Hold on!" cried Perry.

Everyone grabbed hold of the no trespassing sign's post. The meteor cleaved the planet in twain.

As the two halves of the planet drifted apart, David said, "That takes care of the dandelion issue." Then turning toward the water, he said, "Perry?"

Perry and Zaytor looked up to see yet another meteor, which was seconds away from hitting the planet. Everyone's eyes darted from one person to the next.

Perry screamed, "Hang on," yet again.

The meteor crashed into what was left of snake woman's vacation home, blasting it into a million pieces. The three stood holding on tightly to the signpost as they hurtled though space.

The oxygen held by the planet's atmosphere was no more.

Zaytor said, as he exhaled his last breath, "The kettle of fish thing?"

Perry said, "Yup. Definitely the kettle of fish thing."

"Crap," said David.

A PICNIC TO REMEMBER
By Fleur Lind

Rose peddled on her bicycle, her legs well-toned from riding her bike to high school from the family farm a few miles out of town. On wet or wild weather days, she would catch the school bus, but her bike was her pride and joy; the red paintwork gleamed in the sunshine. Rose diligently cleaned the wheels and framework every week or whenever she couldn't avoid riding through a muddy puddle. She gave her bike the same respect as an expensive car.

Joe was her go-to for any mechanical problems. He owned a garage in town, was highly reputable and charged Rose a special rate. He and Rose's father, Ken, had been best mates since their school days, so whatever it took to keep Ken's only daughter safe on the road, Joe would oblige. Joe had recently oiled the chain and cogs too, so that annoying squeak was gone.

Rose's date, Bill, hadn't noticed any squeaks; he was too busy admiring her in a pretty, yellow dress and sneakers.

Bill's old bike was no longer safe to ride as the tiny patch of rust on the handlebar had refused to sleep, and a spring had gone in the seat, making any trip a trifle uncomfortable when going over bumps. To be rid of that prickly feeling on potholes, he had bought a new bike. He was proud of his latest set of wheels and wanted his date with Rose to be perfect, so he was hoping his bike would impress. The teenagers had been picnicking at Mermaid Beach on the Gold Coast and were cycling back to town, with the leftovers of the picnic hamper in the front basket of Rose's bike.

Bill's father, Jim, owned the hardware store in town, and Bill, known for his one-liner jokes and his wacky sense of humor, was always working on his repertoire of corny new material. It was September 1945, and life had been very hard due to rationing and the absence of loved ones who were overseas, so there was often a need to make people laugh, and the locals took it as a tonic. However, on this day, while on their romantic picnic, they were oblivious to a hugely significant event. They were too absorbed in their chatter and Bill's bad jokes.

"Dad's got a new type of broom in stock at the shop, it's selling like hot cakes. You could say its popularity is sweeping the nation!"

Rose giggled. "That is one of your best yet, Bill! Your customers must come in specially to get their daily dose of your jokes."

"I'm glad you liked it, and I hope the customers do. Dad says they are not to encourage me! I'm glad I make people laugh, though. You want some more?"

"Yes, of course! Go on, do some more!"

"Okay then… Did you know that the physics teacher at our high school, Mr. Miller, didn't get on at all well with the biology teacher, Miss Davis?"

"Really? I didn't know that! I thought they did. Why ever not? Did they give each other filthy looks or something?"

"No, but there was no chemistry."

"Aww, Bill!"

"You know what? This Halloween, we should make a scarecrow. My neighbor did one last year, and his scarecrow won an award."

"Did he? Why was that?"

He was outstanding in his field!"

Rose laughed out loud, rolling her eyes. "They are all so good!"

Bill blushed. The best way to win the heart of a young lady was through laughter, regardless of how bad the jokes were.

As they cycled along towards town, they heard a noise that grew louder as they approached the central business district.

The noise was getting louder, but it didn't sound like one of distress or calamity. There was a lot of shouting, and car horns were blaring. Their curiosity grew as they approached.

"What's that noise all about?"

"I don't know."

"Car horns are going mad! I wonder what's going on?"

Bill shrugged, "I don't know, but I hope whatever it is, it isn't bad. We don't need any fighting or aggression in our town; there is enough of it happening with the war."

As they turned onto the main street, the town was in an uproar! People were out on footpaths, cars stopped in their tracks, and dogs barked with excitement as people cheered, clapped, and hugged each other. Strangers shook hands, and the town clock chimed to bring in the good news.

They stopped, standing beside their bikes, completely confused by the scene before them. Jim walked up to them with a huge smile.

"What's going on, Dad?"

"It's over, son! The war is over!" Jim squeezed Bill's shoulder.

"What? That is wonderful to hear!" he turned to Rose, "Rose! It's over!"

Rose began to tear up. "That is so good to hear! But we will still need your jokes, Bill, always."

She stood her bike on its stand and hugged Bill, kissing him lightly on the lips.

The war was over, bringing joy and relief. The celebrations continued, and troops and war personnel came home. Daily life took on a new spin as normality returned.

Love can be fickle, and as young hearts do, Rose and Bill went their separate ways. Rose became a teacher, and Bill took over Jim's shop when he retired.

68 years later, Rose sat in her favorite chair. Now in her 80s, she was a widow.

She was planning a holiday with her family at the same beach where she and Bill had dated.

Excitedly, she recalled her first love. She was hoping to see Bill during her stay.

Would he recognize her?

Rose's eyes sparkled. Her body was aged and stooped, and her movements were slow and careful, but her mind was sharp. The years had taken them from teenagers to seniors, from bikes to walking aids, and from wartime to a world of opportunity.

As for matters of the heart, she was filled with hope and the flutter she had felt from that first kiss. Hopefully, Bill would still know some excellent jokes!

THE STARVING BUG

By Alec Sillifant

"In the light of the moon, a little egg lay on a leaf…"

Carl's frown grew steadily deeper as the pause Dave Caldwell, literary and showbiz agent extraordinaire, had initiated, continued.

"Hmm," said Dave, eventually.

"Hmm? What do you mean, hmm?" said Carl. "You've only read the first line and already you're hmming?"

Dave lifted his eyes from the roughly mocked up book. "I'm sorry, what was that you said?"

"You 'hmmed' after the first line. Shouldn't you read the whole book before you start a critical analysis?"

"I have," said Dave, "from cover to cover. It's just…" the agent tugged at his bottom lip, searching for the right words, "…it's from the first line it seems to go wrong."

"Wrong?" said Carl. "What you have in your hand will become a timeless classic. Loved by generations of children."

Dave couldn't suppress a smile. "Forgive me, Carl, but if I had a dollar for every new author I meet who said that…"

"Okay, Mr Big Shot," said Carl, flinging his hands toward the prototype in Dave's possession, "tell me what's wrong with it?"

Dave stared directly into Carl's eyes, assessing if the man had enough spine to take some constructive slagging-off.

"Okay, the caterpillar's egg is on top of the leaf."

"So?"

"So, everyone knows that caterpillars lay their eggs on the underside of leaves."

"Nit-picking," said Carl. "Besides, I could easily change the view of the leaf. What else?"

"As the story progresses, it turns out this caterpillar is a little on the greedy side. He eats his way through a massive amount of food, is that the kind of message we want to send out to kids?"

Carl's mouth dropped open slightly. "What? It's a story about a caterpillar turning into a beautiful butterfly. It teaches children about the wonders of life and…*and*… how they can change, whatever their beginnings, into greater things."

"Really?" said Dave. He flicked forward a few pages and read aloud.

"He was a big, fat caterpillar." Dave looked up. "Big…fat…are they the kind of words we want our children to associate with in a positive way?"

"This is ridiculous," said Carl. "Political correctness gone mad. Would you tell Roald Dahl he can't call his character The Big Fucking Giant?"

"Friendly," said Dave, "Big Friendly Giant."

"Friendly?"

"Yep."

"Oh…but that's beside the point beca-"

"And look at the food groups you recommend," said Dave, as he selected another page. "Chocolate cake, ice cream, lollipops, cherry pie…do you really want to create a nation of type 2 diabetics?"

"I think you're taking this way too literally," said Carl, rubbing the back of his neck in frustration. "We both know a caterpillar wouldn't eat that kind of stuff."

"We both know caterpillar eggs are laid on the underside of a leaf but that didn't stop your maverick attitude."

"I used food that would resonate with kids," said Carl. "Would you rather I'd written, 'On Tuesday he ate through salmon en croute with an asparagus dressing?' That would be ridiculous."

"I doubt you could draw salmon en croute without making it look like three-year-old's idea of a car wreck," muttered Dave.

"Oh, right, now you don't like the artwork either," said Carl, throwing his hands in the air. "First the words, now the pictures."

"No, the artwork is perfect for the text," said Dave smiling.

For a moment, Carl was held dumbstruck by the thickening sarcasm of the silence. "You think my book is shit, don't you? Come on, say it."

"Shit is such a negative word," said Dave, "maybe your focus was a bit off, that's all. I know my focus has gone after looking at these…rough sketches for a while."

Carl stood up and snatched his mock-up from Dave's hands. "You know what, screw you. I'll take my book to another agent. I'm sure they will see the potential."

Dave grinned. "I believe Weight Watchers have a publishing arm, maybe you could try them? Or you could try a company that specialises in art drawn by drunk monkeys?"

Carl flipped Dave the bird and stormed across the office to grab at the door handle.

"Wait," said Dave. "I don't want you to leave feeling bitter, let me at least give you some helpful advice."

He turned his chair round and grabbed a book off the shelves that covered the entire back wall of the office. Facing Carl again, he opened the book.

"Listen to this… 'It only takes two highly trained eighth grade wizards to turn an everyday domestic cat into a rather spiffing BMX bike.'"

Dave closed the publication and looked up. "That's how you start a bestselling children's picture book."

"It'll be a cold day in Hell before I write a single line about magically endowed zit farms. Up yours, pal!" said Carl and made sure he slammed the door good and proper on his exit.

Dave smiled. "Poor deluded fool."

The intercom on his desk buzzed and Dave depressed the red button.

"Yes, Miss Jones?"

"That band are here to see you, Mr Caldwell, The Beatles."

Dave sighed. "Those tone deaf, half-wit, illiterate Scousers?"

"Yes, Mr. Caldwell."

"Send them in," said Dave, "the sooner I get this over with, the sooner we can all get on with our lives."

YOU NEVER KNOW
By Neil Noble

I met a man, from Ireland, some time ago. He was touring the sights in and around Baltimore and Washington. He struck up a conversation when he stopped in at one of my local watering holes in D.C.

"Sightseeing is a 'tirsty' business," was his first comment.

Recognizing his accent, I told him of my many trips to Ireland and how much I enjoyed myself. He left a short time later to re-board his tour bus, but we did stay connected through the internet.

Not long ago, when we happened to be back across the pond, we met for dinner. During the course of our conversation, he mentioned to me the long and troubling history of people disappearing, never to be seen nor heard from again. We discussed, for some time, over several drinks, whether or not this was related to criminal activity, self-induced, or simply bad luck.

The first two are pretty much self-explanatory. The third, well, I have my own theory about that. I spoke my piece and while I don't think my friend was totally convinced, he did not dismiss it entirely. He is Irish, after all. Here's the thing.

When one insults or otherwise harms, whether intentionally or not, one of the 'little people', one never knows what the end result might be. They are a suspicious lot and do try to avoid our kind as much as possible. On occasion, however, our paths happen to cross. We did agree on that.

The first time my wife and I visited Ireland, some 20 plus years ago, we took a bus tour. One of the stops was at Bunratty Castle. Yes, we did the tourist thing and kissed the Blarney Stone. After doing so, we asked and were directed to the local pub. We were the only patrons, I thought. We ordered, received our drinks and chatted about the castle. She told me how scared she was to be on her back, 85 feet above the ground, so as to kiss the stone. There is a steel grate to catch those who faint. There is also a man holding tight to one's ankles. Yes, one is totally and completely open to the elements. I was surprised when I happened to turn to look out a window at the castle, and there, beside me, stood a smallish, older gentleman with snow white hair. He had long sideburns but no beard. His skin was wrinkled, and his fingers gnarled as he leaned on his shillelagh (walking cane).

Recognizing our American accents, he asked, "is this your first trip here?"

"Yes, it is," we replied in unison.

His accent was thick but quite understandable and he was well dressed in his tweed three-piece suit. I also noticed a four-leaf clover in his lapel.

"Why do you wear a clover instead of a flower in your lapel?"

Ignoring my question, he asked, "may I sit with you folks a spell?"

We said, "yes, and may we buy you a drink?"

"Thank you kindly."

He regaled us with some of the lore of the area for nearly an hour. He told us more about the history of the Castle and its famous stone. He was mesmerizing.

Eventually, our bus driver called out, "we'll be leaving in a few minutes."

It was only then that it occurred to me he was relating these stories in the first person. I never got the chance to ask about it.

As we got up, I held out my hand for a shake. His answer was curious.

"I cannot for I want no harm to come to you, but I do wish you well and safe home."

"Well, thank you for the company and stories. And good health and long life to you."

He smiled almost to the point of laughing. Indeed, he seemed to be laughing to himself. We walked out of the pub and right there, at the door sill, was a ten-pound note. I picked it up and stepped back inside but I only saw the barmaid.

I asked the lady, "where did the old gentleman go."

She responded, "who?"

"We were just in here talking to an older gentleman. He was wearing a green tweed suit, had white hair, and carrying a shillelagh. I bought a drink for him. Where did he go?"

"Sorry, Sir. You and your Mrs. were the only two in here most of this afternoon. And you only bought the two drinks."

I stared at her, blinked several times, and looked around the empty room. I thanked her, tipped my hat, and left for the bus. I could hear her behind me as I walked out laughing but I gave it no mind.

When we boarded the bus, we retold the story. Both the driver and tour guide began laughing.

When they calmed down, one said, "They almost never speak to outsiders. You must have been most kind to him."

The tour guide then the described the old man to a tee.

"He approached us because he recognized our accent, and we did buy him a drink. We chatted this whole time we were stopped. He told us stories about some of the history of the castle."

The driver and tour guide laughed some more.

It took more than a few minutes for the realization to sink in as to what we had just witnessed and actually been part of.

"What in blazes, are you going on about? Are you saying what I think you're saying? Was that old man…?"

Amidst their laughter, they nodded.

"Yes, we believe so," said the driver "it doesn't happen often but it's not uncommon. The two of us will have a good laugh at your expense, with our mates, at our own pub, when we retell your story."

So, it always pays to be nice. You never know.

THE STOWAWAY
By Fleur Lind

"Hey Lizzie, happy birthday!" Maxine sang to her sister's face on her phone screen.

A FaceTime chat worked, despite the absence of a physical meeting and hugs.

"Hey Chicky! Thank you! It's a shame you're not here; you should see my cake! It's huge and gorgeous. Danielle has surpassed her cake icing skills this year."

Well, it should be a big cake for your 50th! Well done to Danielle. I knew she would deliver!"

"Thanks so much for organizing it. It makes the distance between us twice as far."

"Never mind, we'll make up for lost time with the next lap around the sun, eh?"

"Remember that epic road trip you did with the kids five years ago? It took me a day or two to stop aching from laughing when you told me about your stowaway."

"Oh, yeah. I remember that so well. Covid was the least of our problems. Getting through the border patrols was a breeze compared to what shared the front seat…"

Five years earlier…

In 2020, the COVID-19 pandemic was making any form of interstate travel challenging or impossible because of hot spots, clusters, and border closures. It was new jargon that became the norm with Covid.

Maxine and her children, plus two, were enticed up to Queensland to visit her sister for part of the school holidays. The lure of the beaches, the warmer weather, and the theme parks were enough to give an unsavory salute to the pandemic and do a road trip from their rural setting in New South Wales to the sunny north. But all was not as it seemed.

Simon squinted with distaste as he listened to the ongoing whiny sound emanating from a carload of smelly teenagers. The long drive was tiresome, but he couldn't complain, having hitched a ride for 626 kilometers. As much as he wanted to give them all something to whine about, he was safe and comfortable on the floor, unnoticed under the front passenger seat. The driver and five passengers were oblivious to his presence.

"How much longer, Mum? I'm hungry."

"I'm bored. There's no coverage; we're in a dead zone."

"That sounds like a line from a zombie movie."

"My phone's flat."

"Use your battery pack…"

"I couldn't find it, so I didn't pack it."

"Well, maybe you should tidy your room more often, bro."

"You can talk; your room is worse than mine."

"Is not!"

"I've got a cramp in my leg, and my bum's numb…"

"Clay, did you change your socks before we left home? Your feet smell rotten!"

"Uh…oops."

"Ew…who dropped that one?"

"That's so gross!"

"Oh my god, I need air!"

"Don't look at me, it was him!"

With her left hand on the steering wheel, the other hand cradling her head against the ledge of her door by the partially open window, Maxine cursed the rotten timing when the aircon went on the blink halfway to the border.

She pressed the button on her door to open the electric windows for the rear of her dated 7-seater van. She quietly questioned her sanity about the moment she had agreed to take her three teenage kids, plus two friends, on a school holiday excursion to the Sunshine State. It had seemed like a good idea escaping the drought doldrums in their small rural town in NSW, to have a break with her sister in Noosa on the Sunshine Coast of Queensland.

Go on a road trip, they said. It'll be fun, they said. Maxine rolled her eyes. But regardless of the imminent hassles, they packed all they needed for the trip, both essentials and luxuries, whatever it took to keep their carload of grizzly campers content for their journey.

Her sense of humor had waned after just three hours of driving, despite the comfort stops. A niggly thought in the back of Maxine's mind was the horror of not getting across the border. She had the correct paperwork, but as tiredness began to overtake any rational thinking, she started overthinking scenarios of being told to turn around and go back. She had seen it happen on the evening news; it looked daunting and horrifying. To go all that way, to be told to turn back. She couldn't bear it if that happened. She didn't drink alcohol, not even a tipple, but she doubted the Diet Coke packed in the cooler bag was going to help if her paperwork didn't meet the criteria.

Simon, on the other hand, was content. He would have preferred some quiet to nap, but as that small luxury was not likely to eventuate, he would remain cool and calm in his curled-up state.

Despite a few more skirmishes from the teens; ongoing grizzles, and small pesky problems such as encroaching on personal space, odor and flatulence, someone losing a game on their phone, someone snoring and dribbling, and the all-consuming irregularity of phone coverage making any device activity blip off the radar until a signal was available again… the road trip to the Queensland border went as harmoniously as it could with five bored teenagers.

Maxine had the radio on, but there were arguments about the best station to listen to until the speakers issued an annoying static crackle, indicating lost reception. She missed having a CD player, like their surround sound system at home, but sadly, her car was an older model without such frills and benefits.

Her next car would be a smaller one, she mused, with all the mod cons, when the kids don't need transporting here, there, and everywhere. They'll have their licenses and their cars.

Snapping out of her thoughts, Maxine flicked her attention from the road ahead to the dashboard at regular intervals, feeling her euphoria build as the GPS advised her of the shrinking distance left to travel.

With the border just a few kilometers away, the cold, hard reality of how many other travelers were hopeful of heading north was like hitting a brick wall. The queue of stationary cars, drivers waiting to have their paperwork checked and the mandatory COVID-19 test completed, was difficult to comprehend. Her earlier euphoria dissipated like a popped bubble. After what felt like a waiting time of as long as it had taken to drive from their home, there was a movement with one PPE-clad official bending over to talk to Maxine through her open car window.

Simon lifted his head, and with his small eyes wide open, his senses were aware of a change in his environment. The car was still, the swerving from changing lanes or overtaking and turning corners had stopped, and there was no more sudden decrease in speed causing him to move about from his comfortable position, but the vibration of the engine was still happening.

He heard other voices apart from the whiny teens. The driver had stopped snapping at her passengers but was thinking out loud as she prepared her paperwork. Another voice sounded friendly, but official. There was a shuffle of papers, questions asked, answers given, a brief exchange of conversation, and the tests were duly completed on each passenger. One of the teens stated how disgusting and weird it was having something pushed so far up their nose and then pulled back out again; it gave her a brief burning sensation and made her eyes water.

The engine's rumble increased as the car moved back into gear and followed the traffic. Simon was fully alert now, thinking another comfort stop must be around the corner. That would be his exit point.

And indeed, it was. The doors opened, allowing fresh air to blow in on the warm breeze. This was pure relief for Simon, who had had to deal with foot odor as well as flatulence from fellow passengers. With the occupants legging it to the rest area ablution, Simon started to uncurl. Perhaps a stretch across the seat might be wise before heading onto the dry grass on the roadside.

At that moment, with just two toilets making it necessary to queue, one of the teens turned and ran back to the car to get her phone. After all, she didn't want to miss anything important in the five minutes she would not have it in her pocket. Simon was too busy enjoying his stretch to notice Lillian heading straight for her phone, which was underneath him.

"SNAKE!" Lillian screamed, turning white with fear.

"Bloody hell!" Maxine yelled from inside the toilet cubicle.

"Really? Where?" Tim was getting out his phone.

"ON MY SEAT!"

"What is it? A Brown?"

"A BIG ONE!" Was all Lillian could offer in her terrified state.

All but Rory and Grace, who were inside their respective cubicles answering the call of nature, ran toward the car.

"Get away from the car! Step away from the car!" Maxine yelled, while zipping her fly on her jeans as she ran toward Lillian.

This commotion was all too much for Simon, who had reared up from the seat, his mouth open, feeling as shocked as those staring at him.

There was only one thing to do. Get out of the car, *fast!* With one fluid, slick motion, his two-meter-long body slithered off the phone, off the seat, out the passenger door and onto the comforting green grass of the rest area.

Simon didn't look back; he was gone. In his wake, he left five startled teens, and Maxine, who had forgotten about the border, and was feeling that need for something stronger than the Diet Coke she had packed in the cooler bag. A double-shot cappuccino would do nicely right about now.

"Ohh! He was *HUGE!*"

"I got a great photo!"

"He was sitting on my phone! Eeeeww!!"

"You'd better sanitize it then! I'm doing Insta! and Facebook!"

"I'm doing a post! And Snapchat! Tag me!"

As her hands trembled, Maxine rolled her eyes as she took a few deep breaths to calm down. How and *when* did a snake *that* size get in the car? That was a close call and ticked all the hazardous boxes for their road trip to potentially go terribly wrong in the middle of nowhere. Imagine if any, or all of them had been bitten. Maxine shuddered and tried to erase the thought. But there was an upside. The slithery stowaway would be just the diversion she needed to occupy the kids for the last stretch of the road trip.

Simon was well pleased. He was feeling joyous as he slithered along, having crossed the border without question. And even more satisfying, he had paid back those whiny kids. Hours of noise, travelling, and smell can leave a lasting effect on a snake.

It had been a bumpy ride, but a safe passage north. Now, to reunite with his Eastern Brown community in Queensland. Job done!

To Be Continued

The NobleJay Collection

Volume 3

is COMING SOON!

To be released Spring 2026

www.ingramcontent.com/pod-product-compliance
Lightning Source LLC
Chambersburg PA
CBHW031258170626
46807CB00001B/211